**Dear parents, caregivers, and educators:**

If you want to get your child excited about reading, you've come to the right place! Ready-to-Read *GRAPHICS* is the perfect launchpad for emerging graphic novel readers.

All Ready-to-Read *GRAPHICS* books include the following:

★ **A how-to guide to reading graphic novels for first-time readers**

★ **Easy-to-follow panels to support reading comprehension**

★ **Accessible vocabulary to build your child's reading confidence**

★ **Compelling stories that star your child's favorite characters**

★ **Fresh, engaging illustrations that provide context and promote visual literacy**

Wherever your child may be on their reading journey, Ready-to-Read *GRAPHICS* will make them giggle, gasp, and want to keep reading more.

*Blast off on this starry adventure . . . a universe of graphic novel reading awaits!*

# RED TITAN
## AND THE RUNAWAY ROBOT

### SIMON SPOTLIGHT

An imprint of Simon & Schuster Children's Publishing Division
1230 Avenue of the Americas, New York, New York 10020
This Simon Spotlight edition September 2021
Text by Arie Kaplan

For more information about special discounts for bulk purchases, please contact
Simon & Schuster Special Sales at 1-866-506-1949 or business@simonandschuster.com.
Manufactured in the United States of America 0821 LAK
2 4 6 8 10 9 7 5 3 1
ISBN 978-1-6659-0179-6 (hc)
ISBN 978-1-6659-0178-9 (pbk)
ISBN 978-1-6659-0180-2 (ebook)

# RED TITAN
## AND THE RUNAWAY ROBOT

by **RYAN KAJI**
written by **ARIE KAPLAN**
illustrated by **PATRICK SPAZIANTE**

Ready-to-Read *GRAPHICS*

Simon Spotlight
New York   London   Toronto   Sydney   New Delhi

# HOW TO READ THIS BOOK

Ryan is here to give you some tips on reading this book.

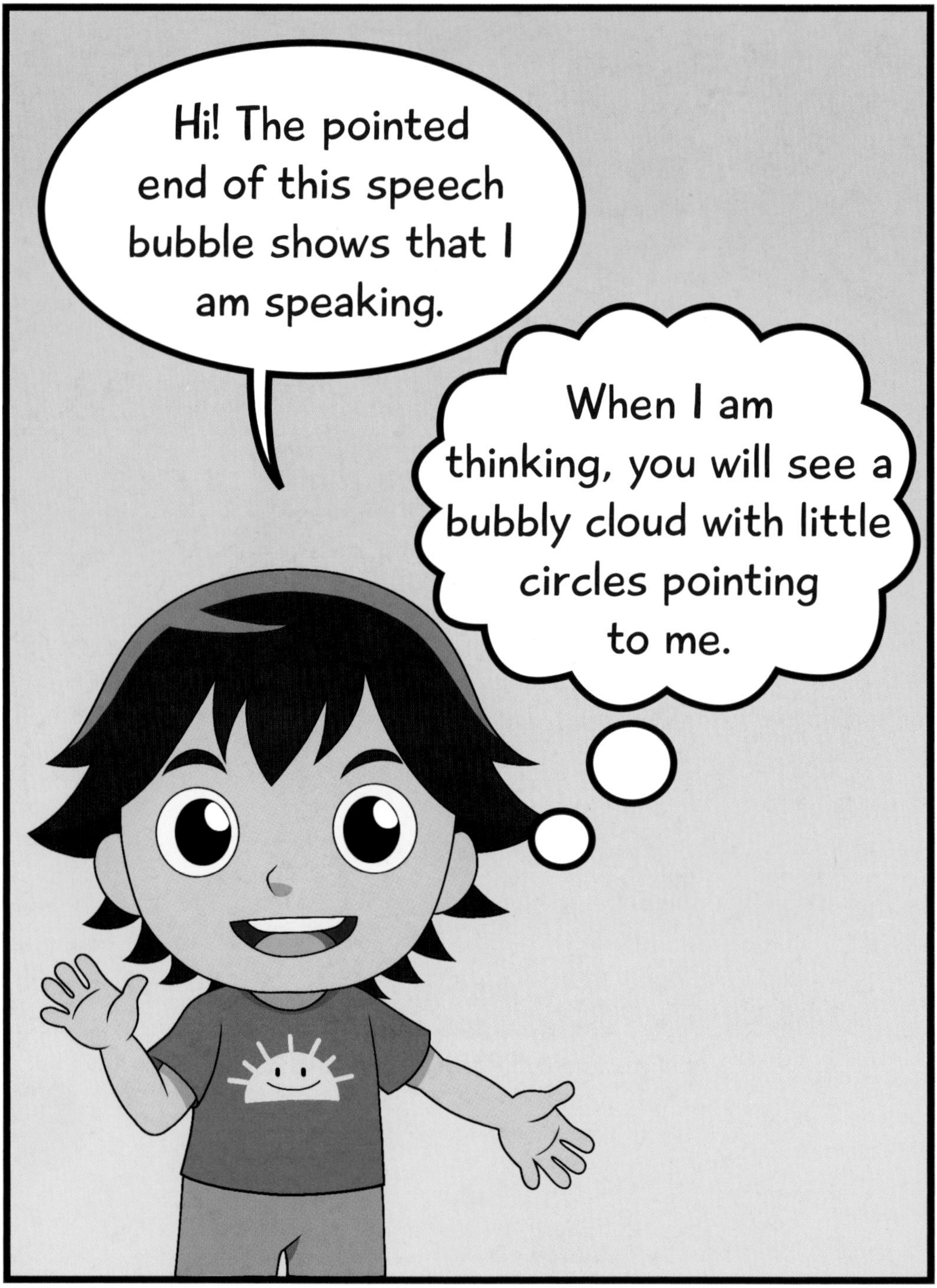
Hi! The pointed end of this speech bubble shows that I am speaking.
When I am thinking, you will see a bubbly cloud with little circles pointing to me.

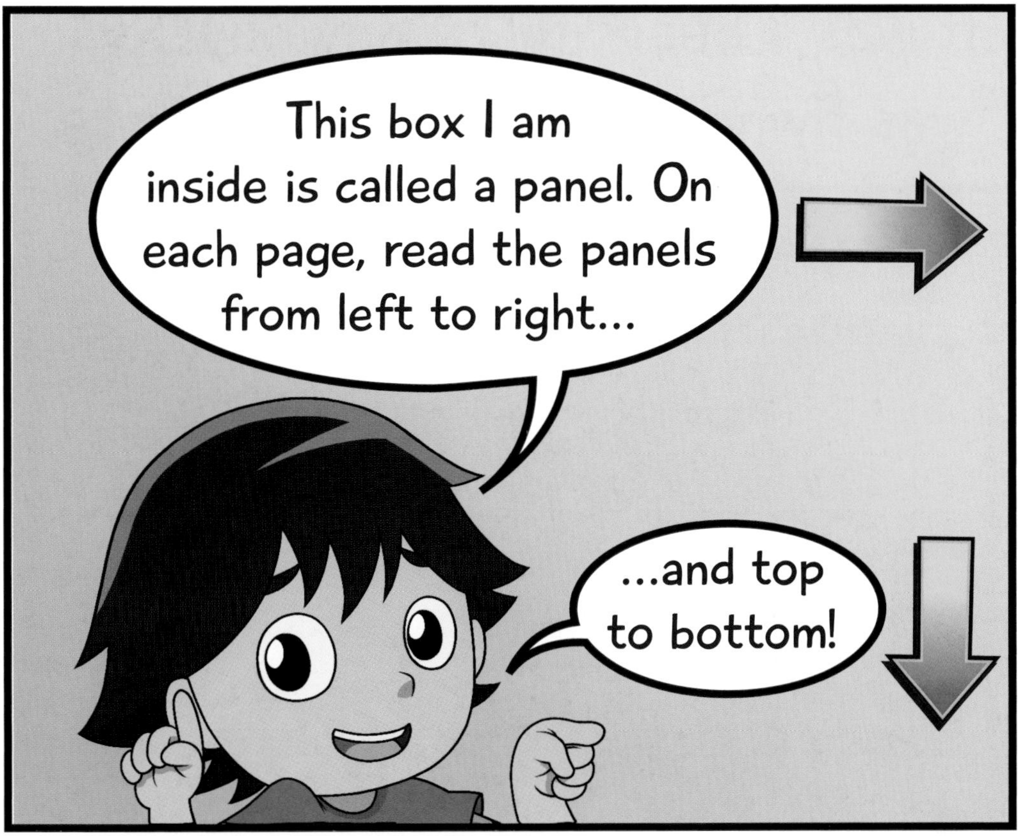
This box I am inside is called a panel. On each page, read the panels from left to right...
...and top to bottom!

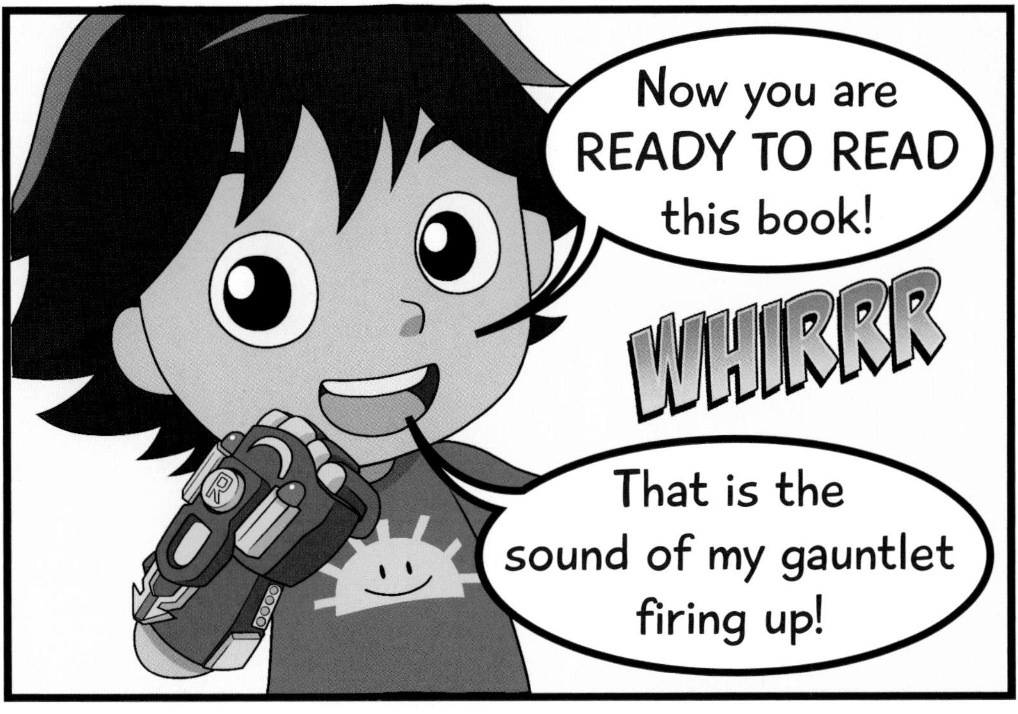
Now you are READY TO READ this book!
WHIRRR
That is the sound of my gauntlet firing up!

It was a beautiful, sunny day. Ryan was flying a kite with his parents.

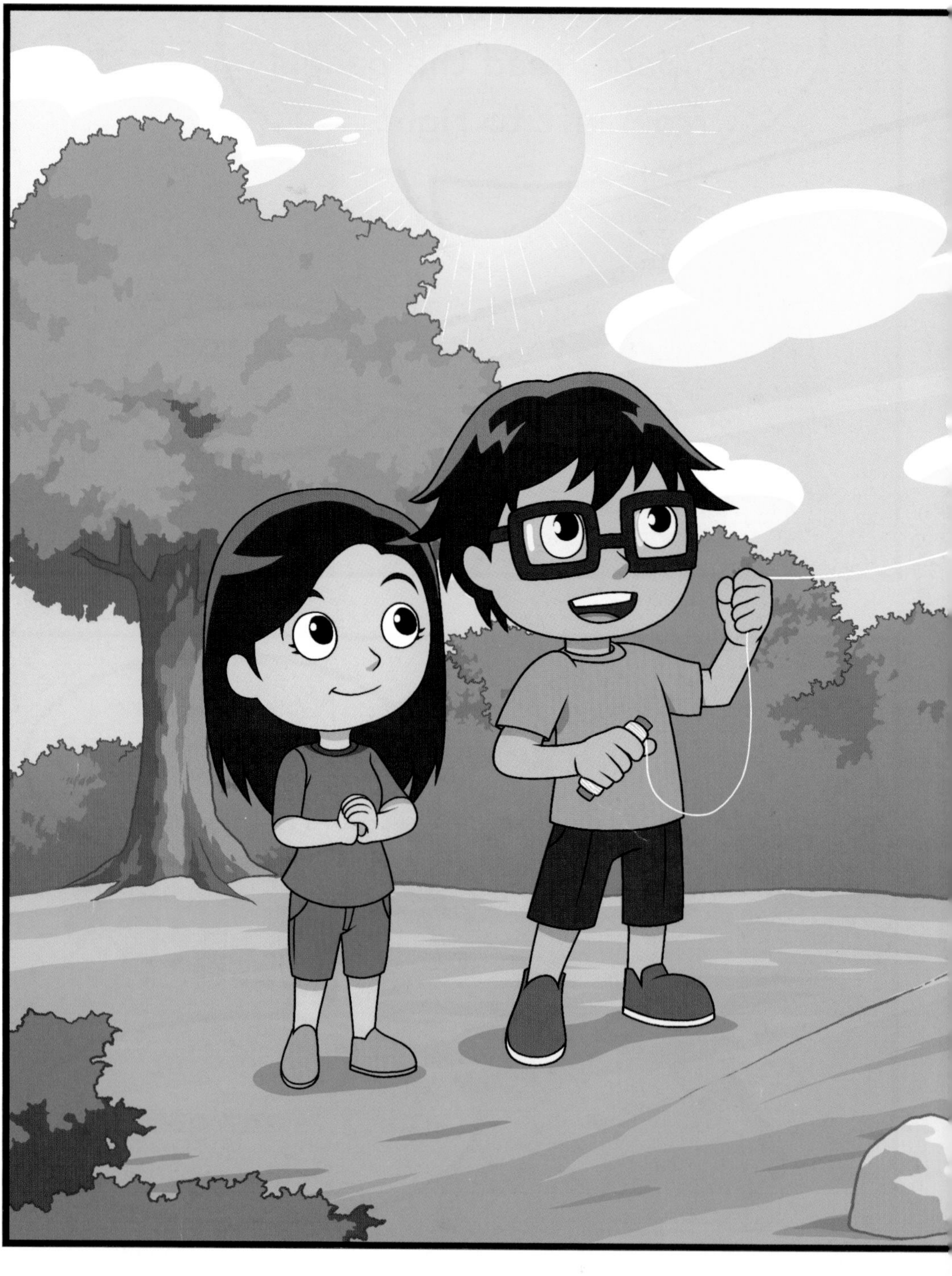

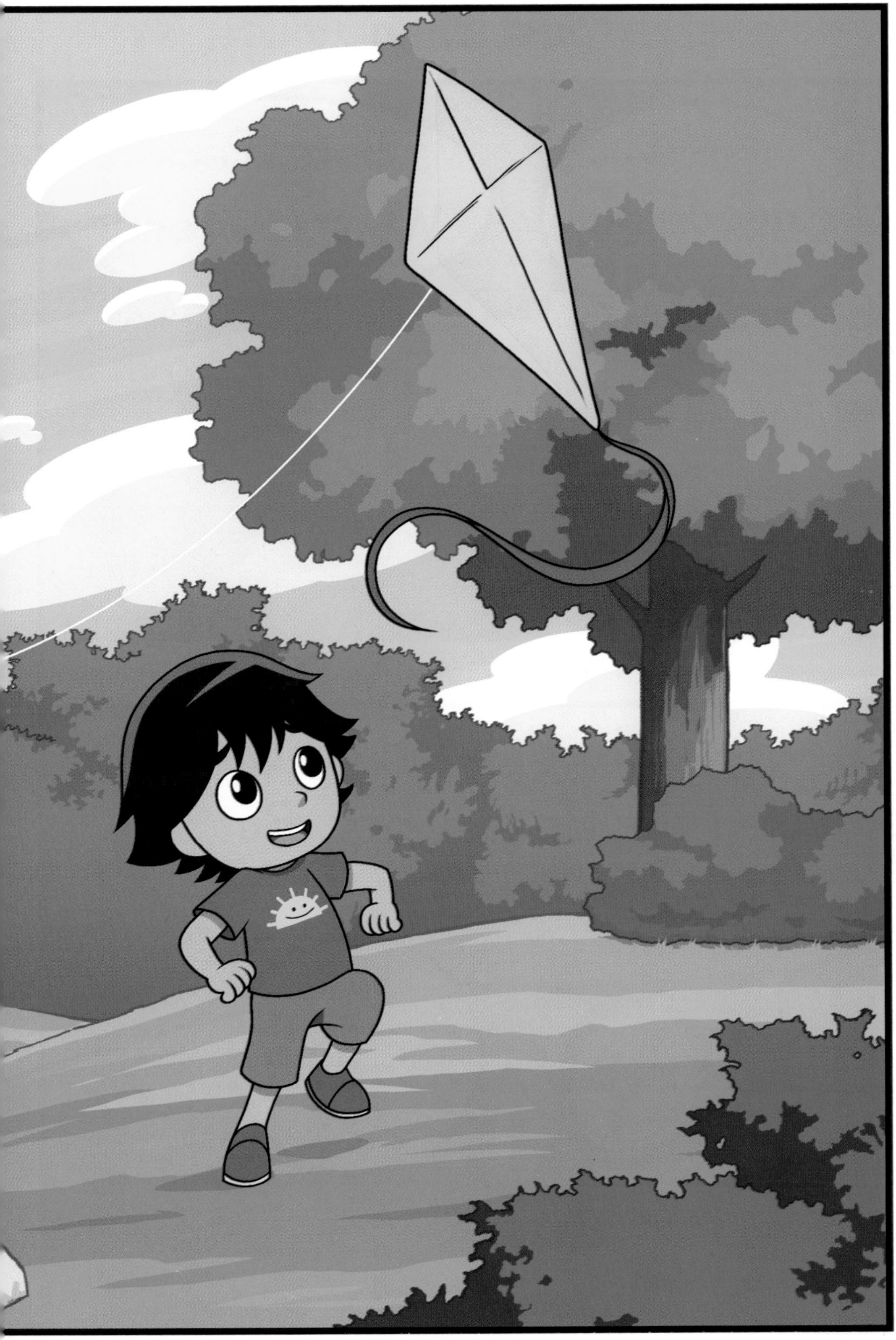

Just then...

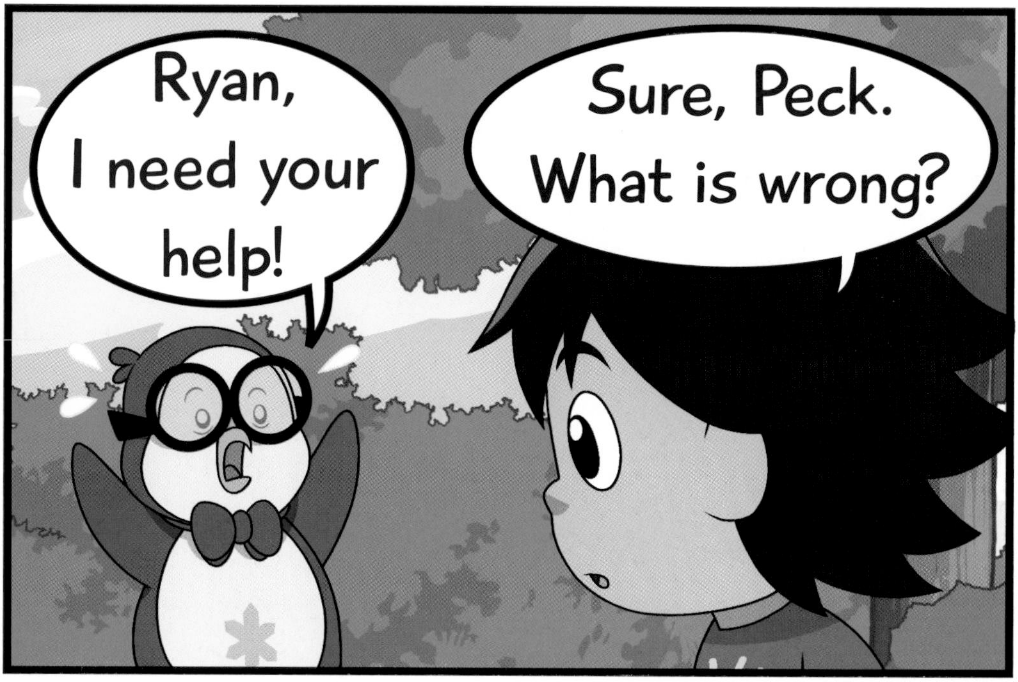

Ryan, I need your help!
Sure, Peck. What is wrong?


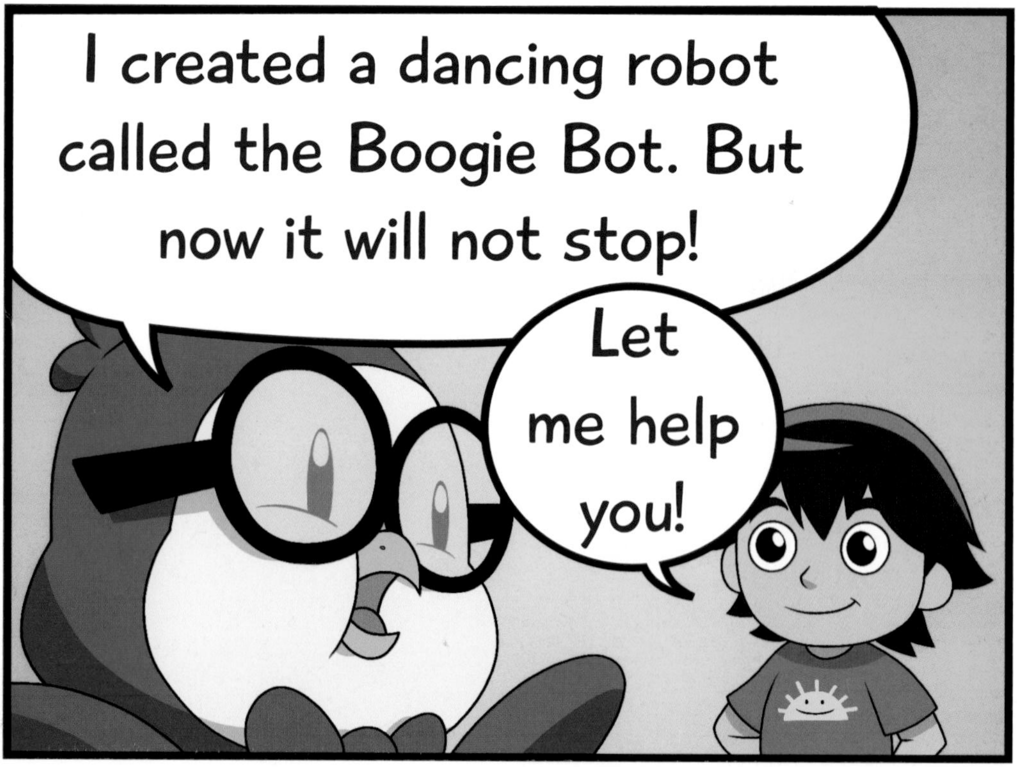

I created a dancing robot called the Boogie Bot. But now it will not stop!
Let me help you!

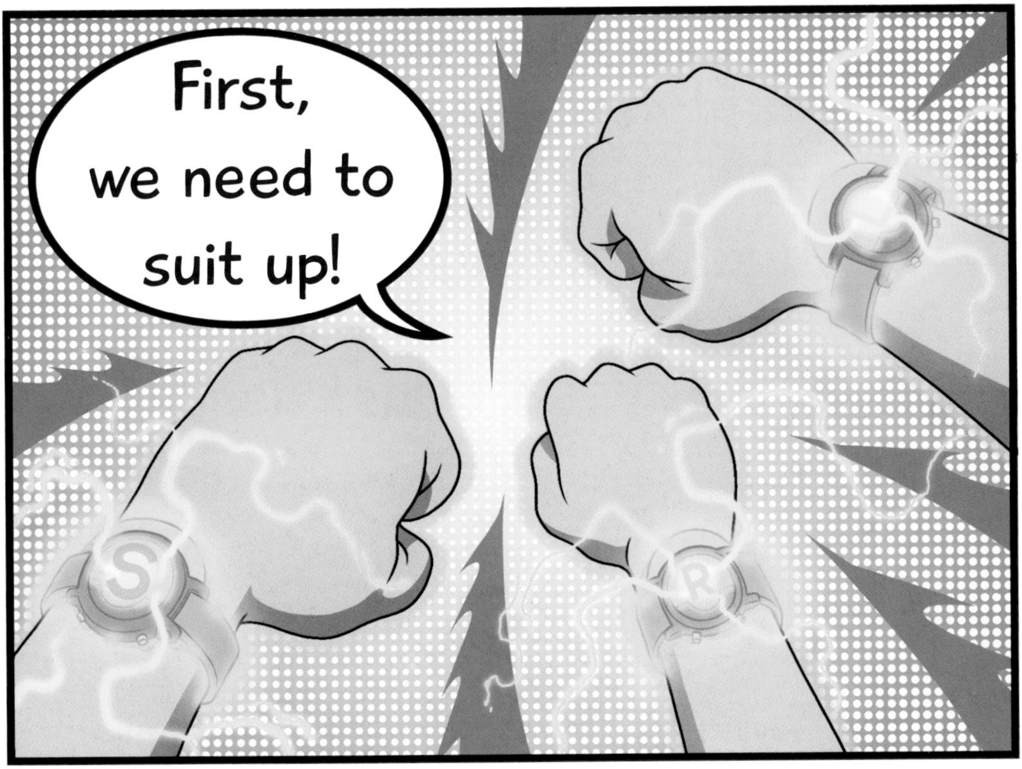
First, we need to suit up!

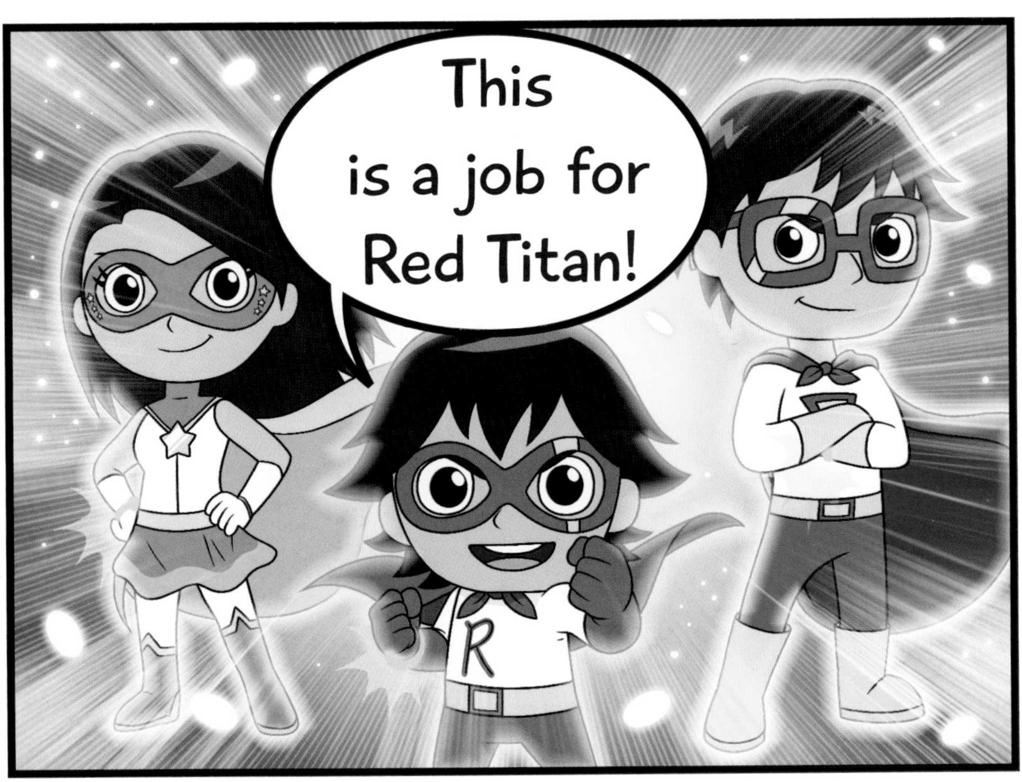
This is a job for Red Titan!
R

Moments later, at the lab...

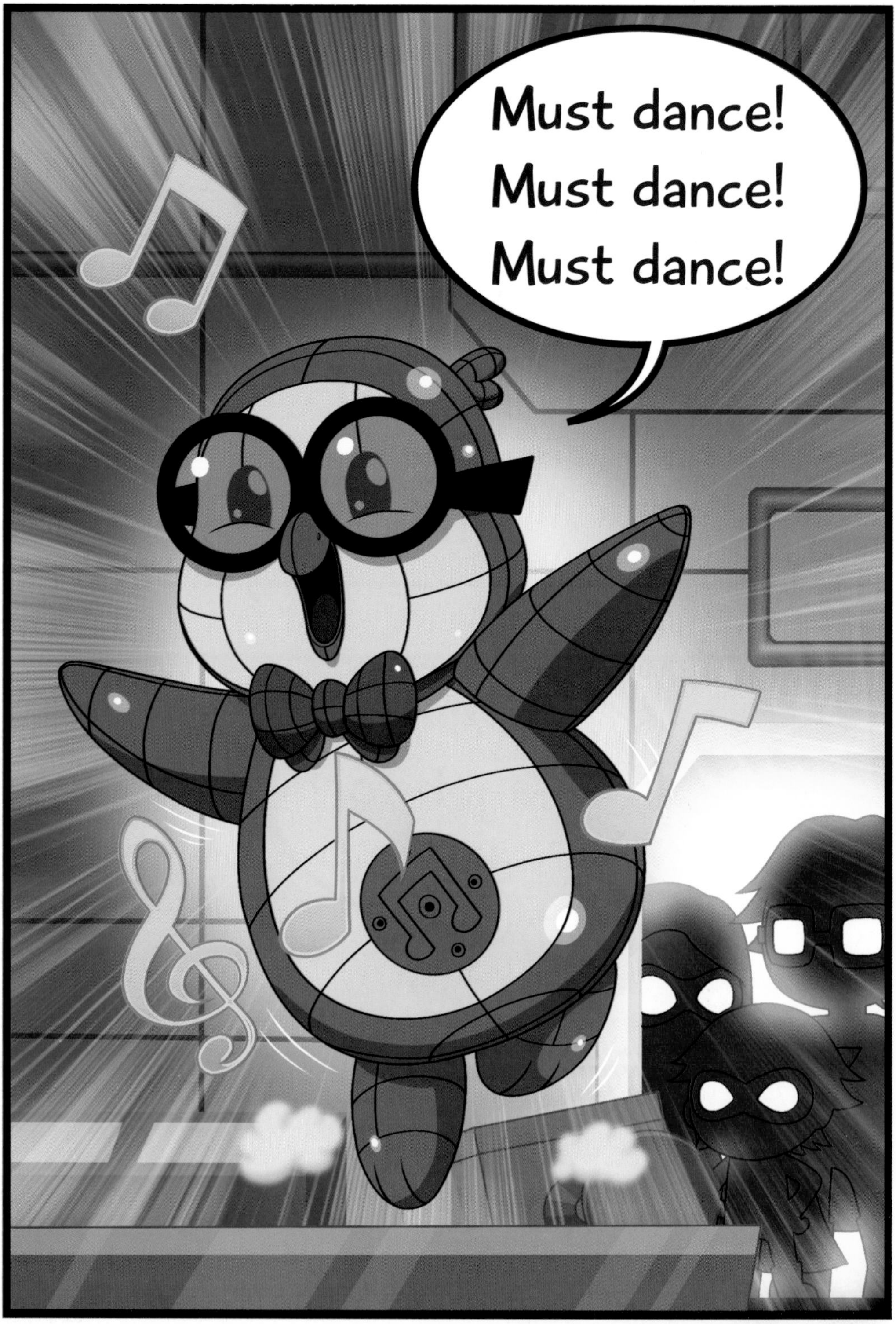
Must dance!
Must dance!
Must dance!

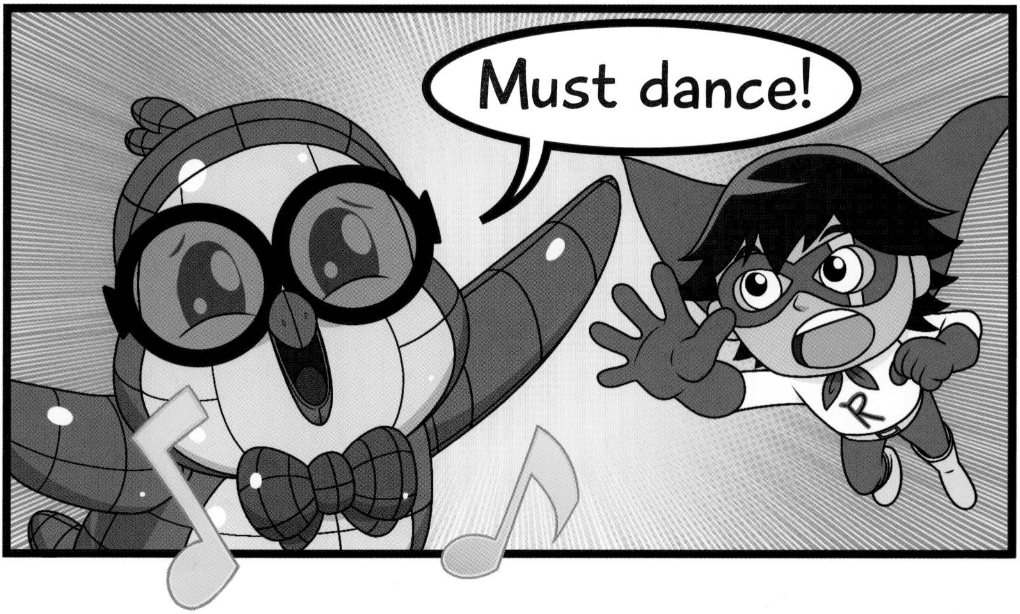
Must dance!

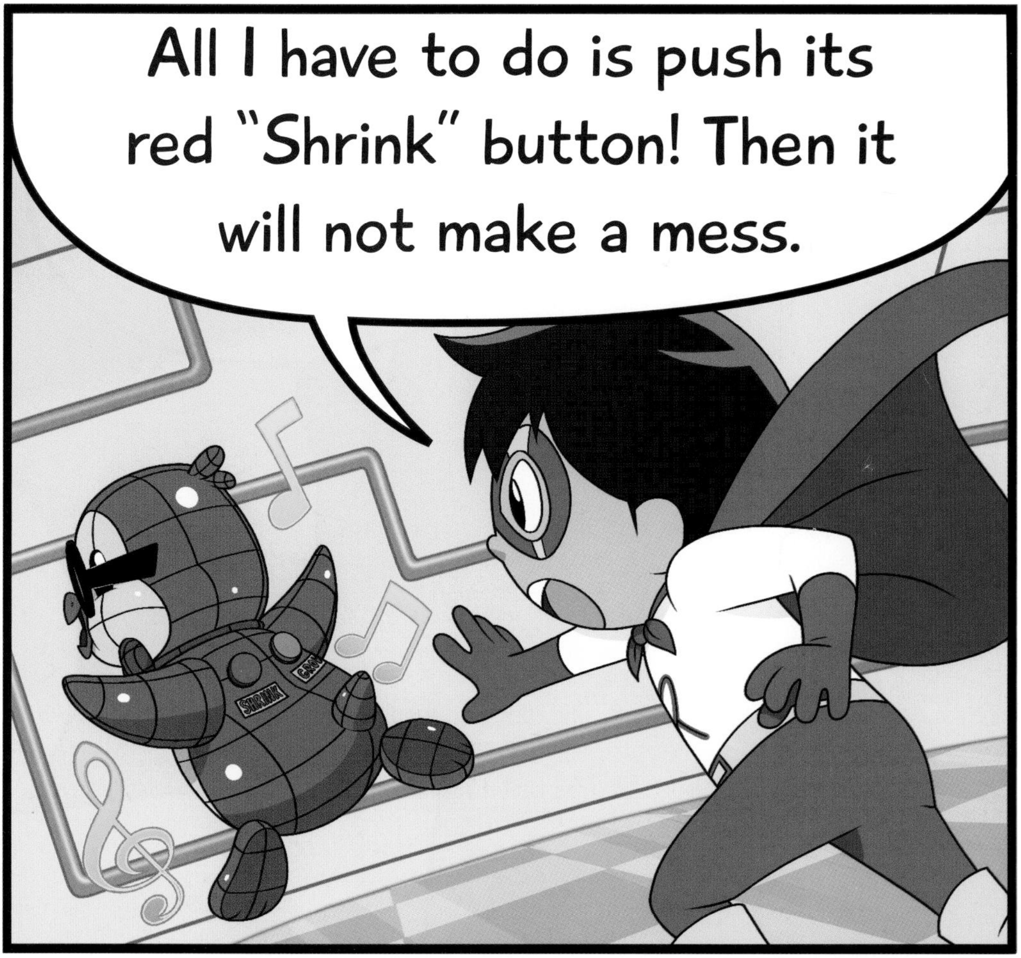
All I have to do is push its red "Shrink" button! Then it will not make a mess.
SHRINK

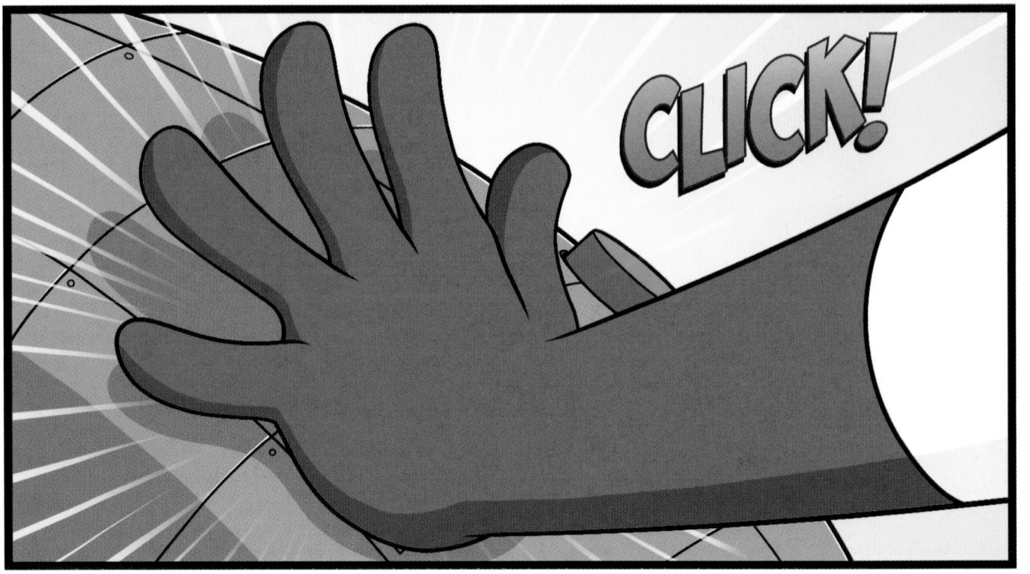
CLICK!

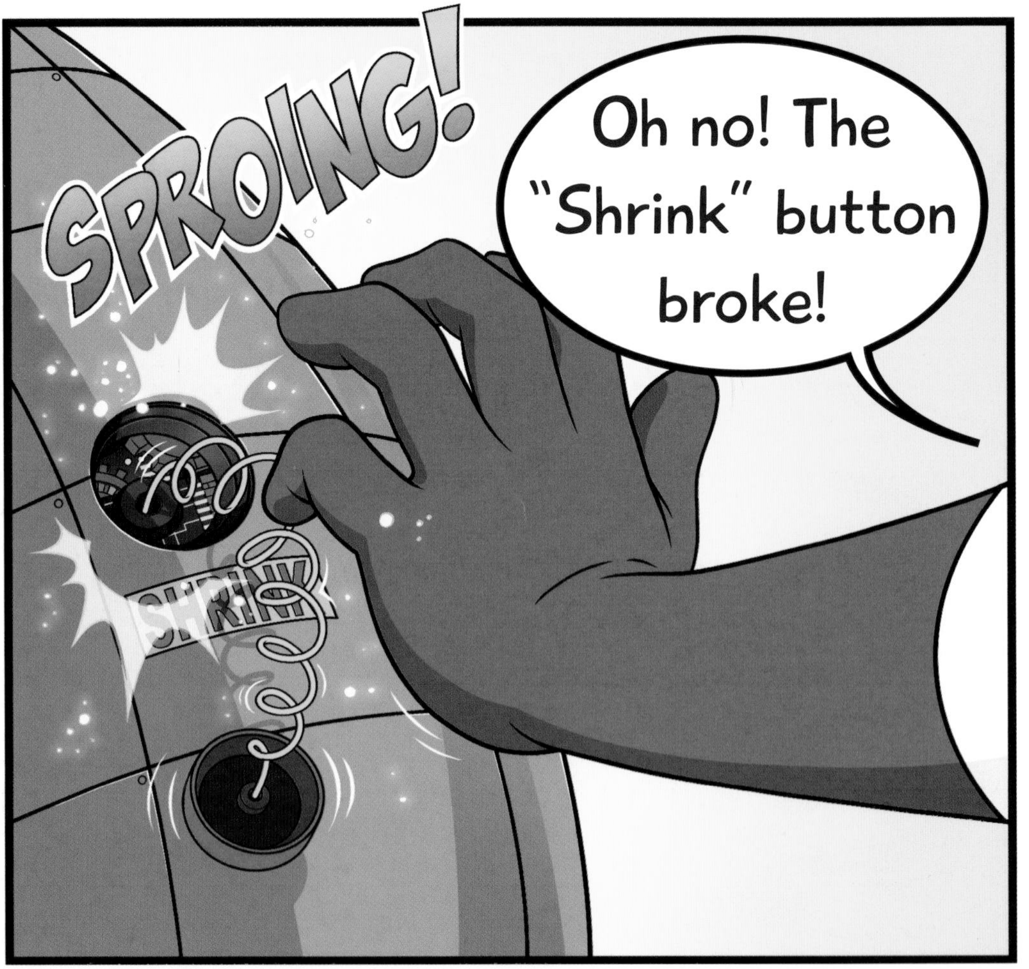
SPROING!
Oh no! The "Shrink" button broke!
SHRINK

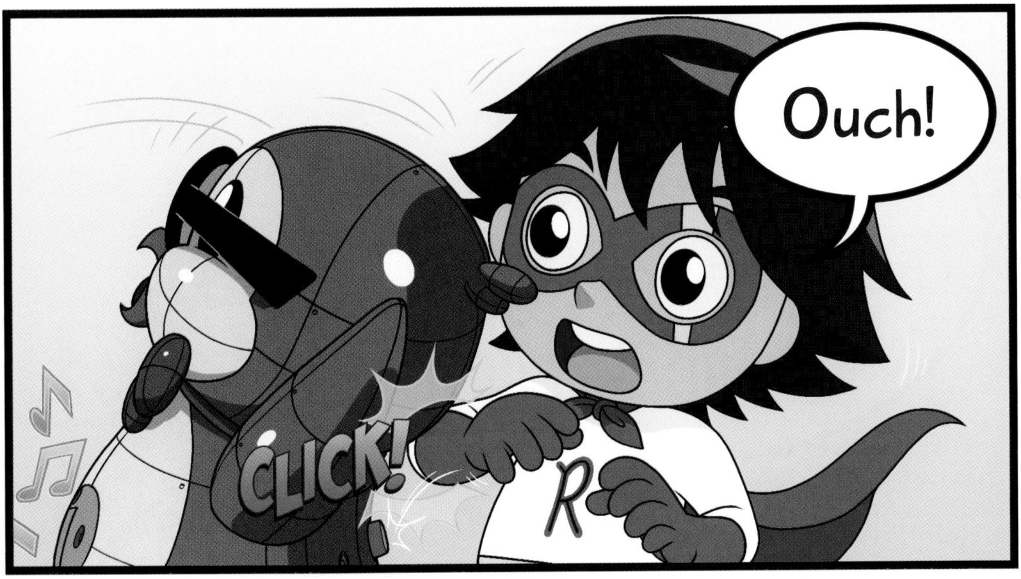
Ouch!
CLICK!

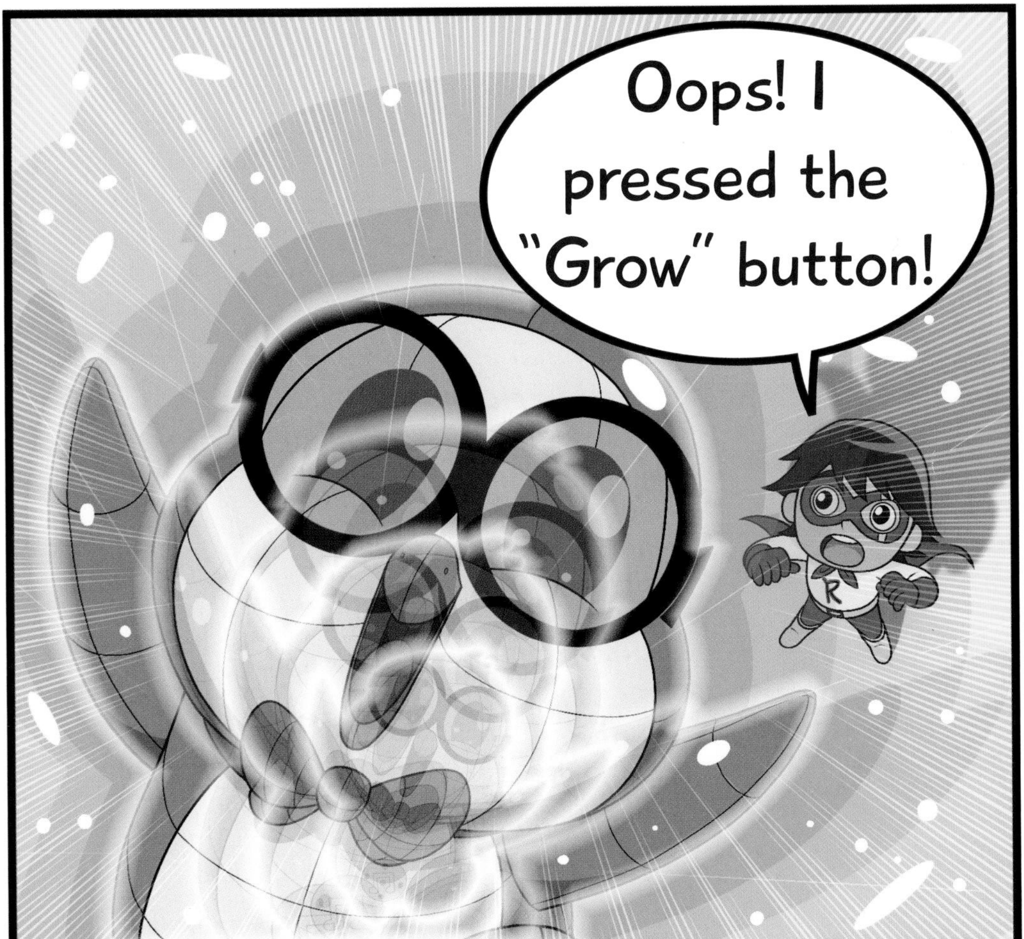
Oops! I pressed the "Grow" button!

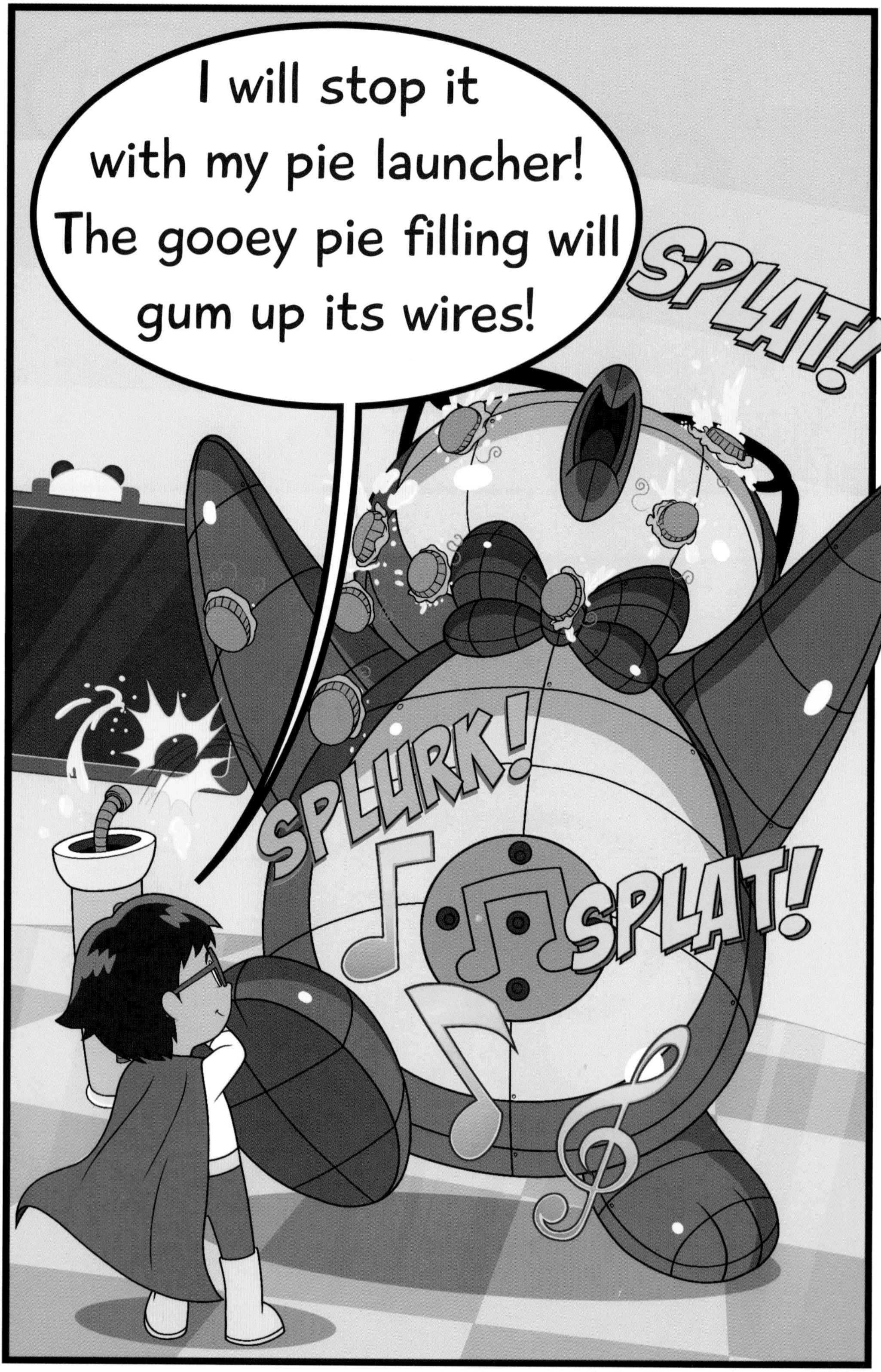
I will stop it with my pie launcher! The gooey pie filling will gum up its wires!
SPLAT!
SPLURK!
SPLAT!

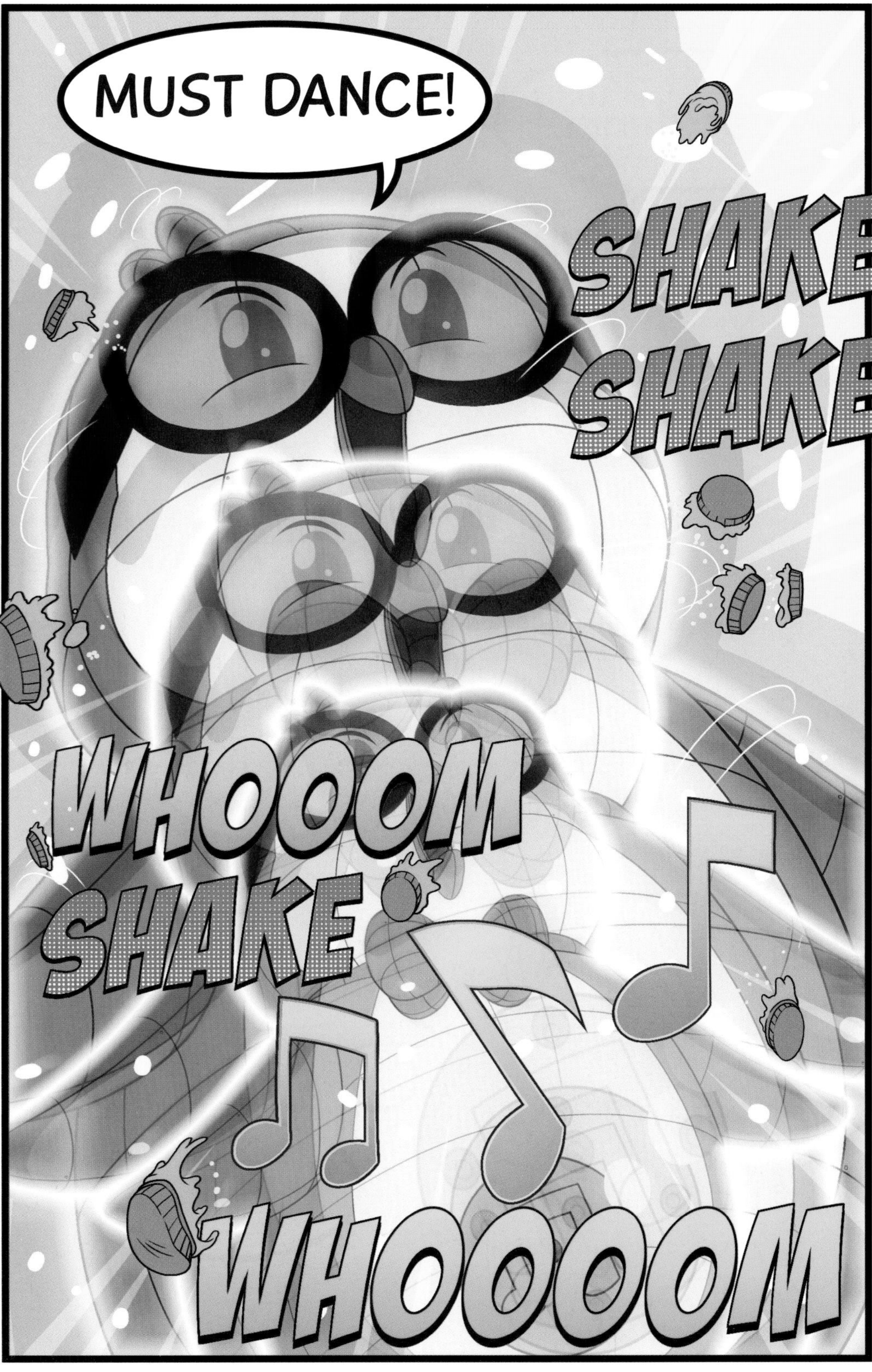
MUST DANCE!
SHAKE
SHAKE
WHOOOM
SHAKE
WHOOOOM

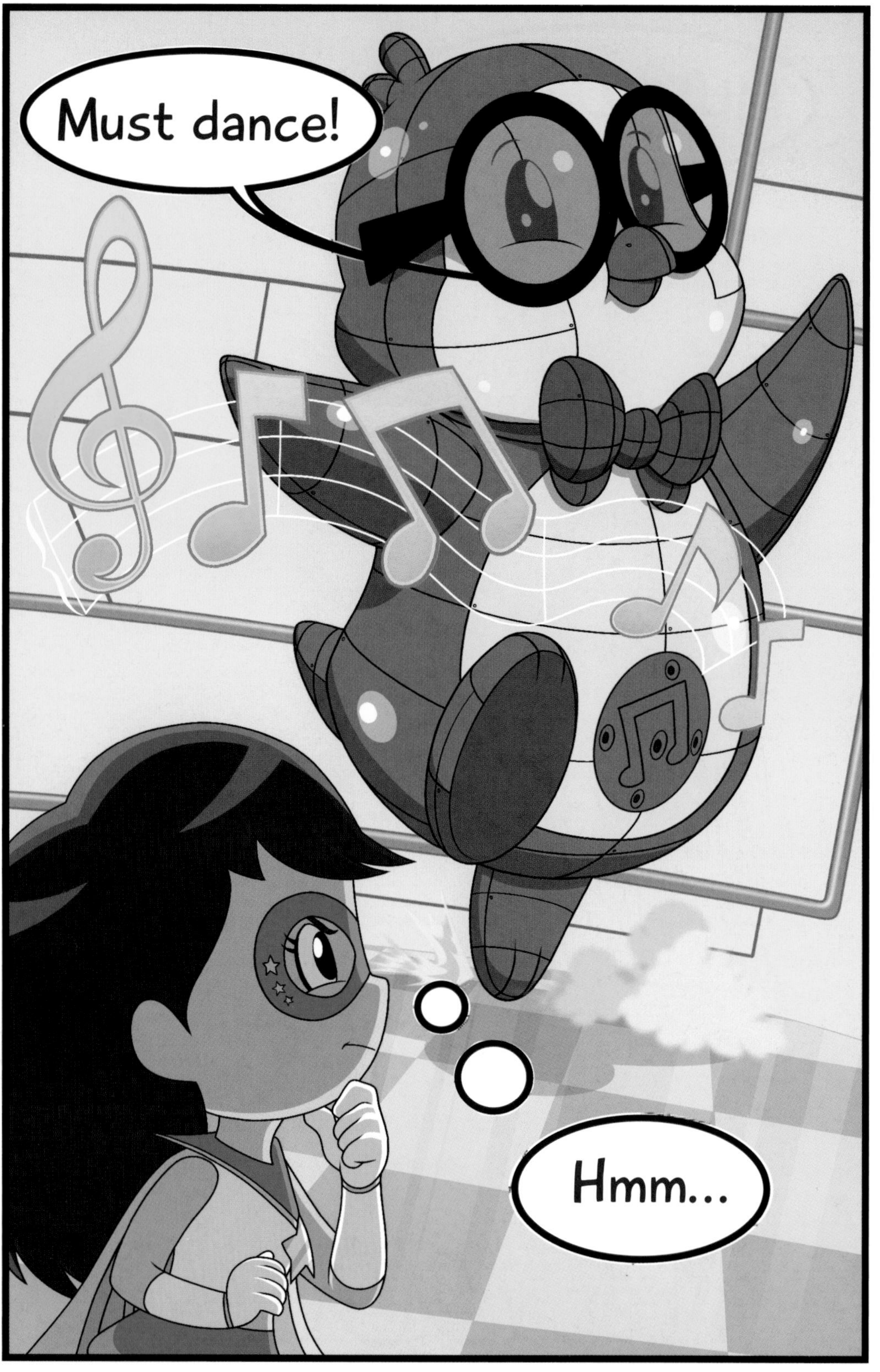
Must dance!
Hmm...

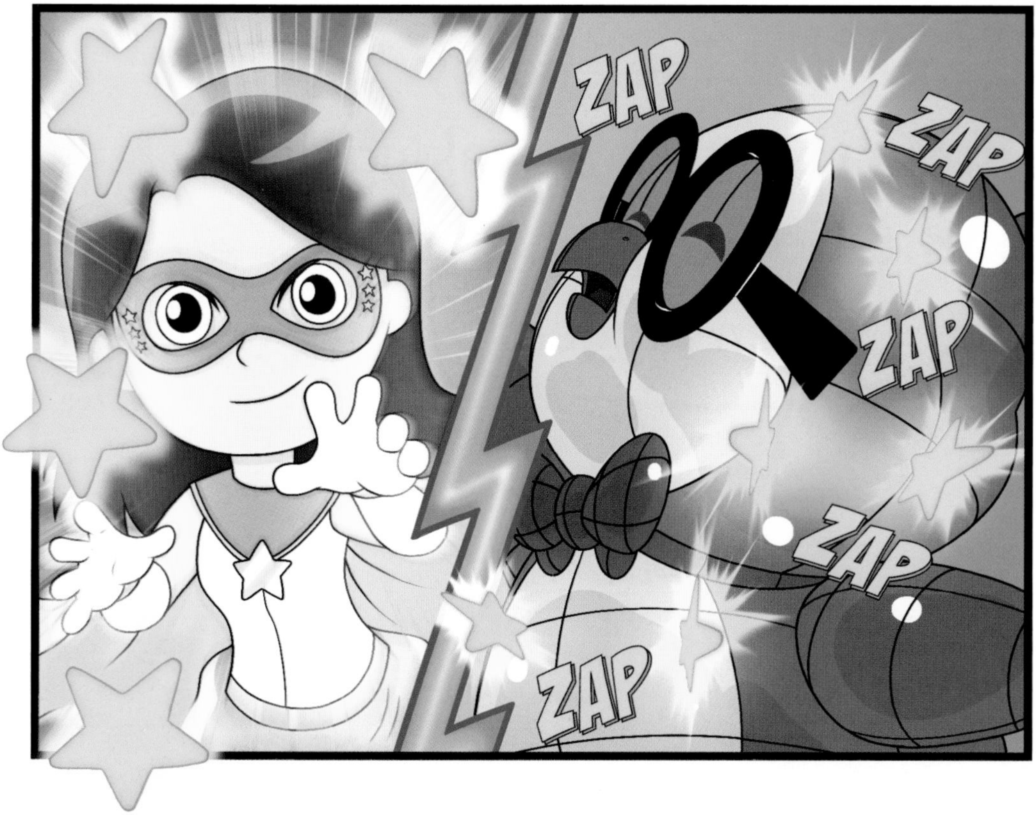
ZAP
ZAP
ZAP
ZAP
ZAP

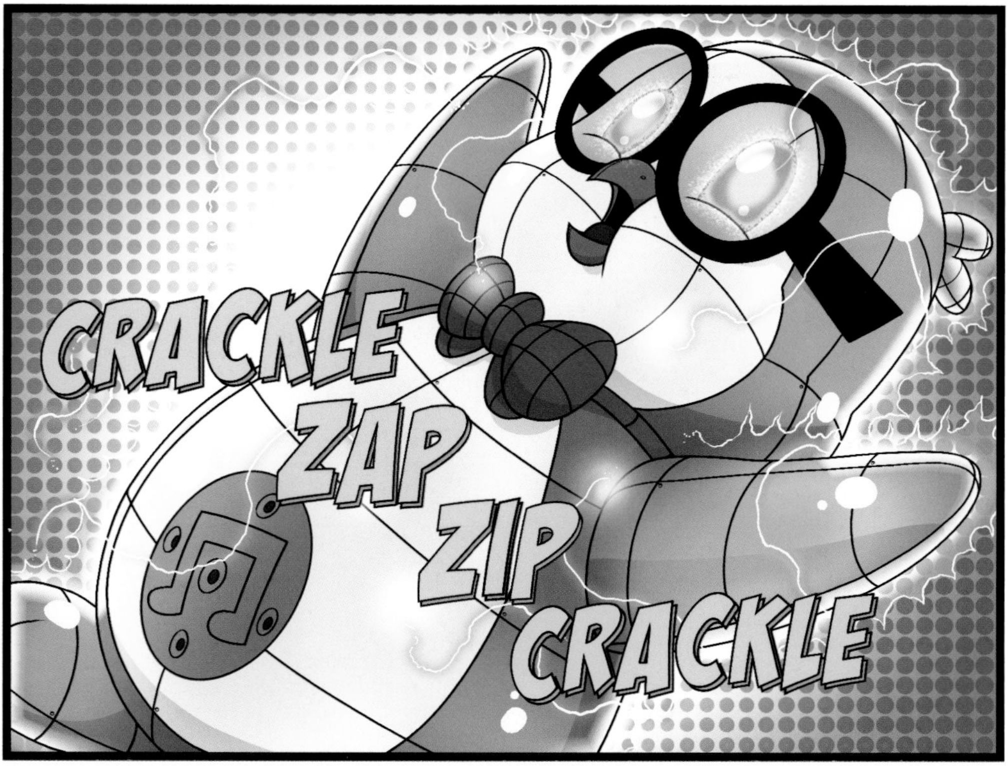
CRACKLE
ZAP
ZIP
CRACKLE

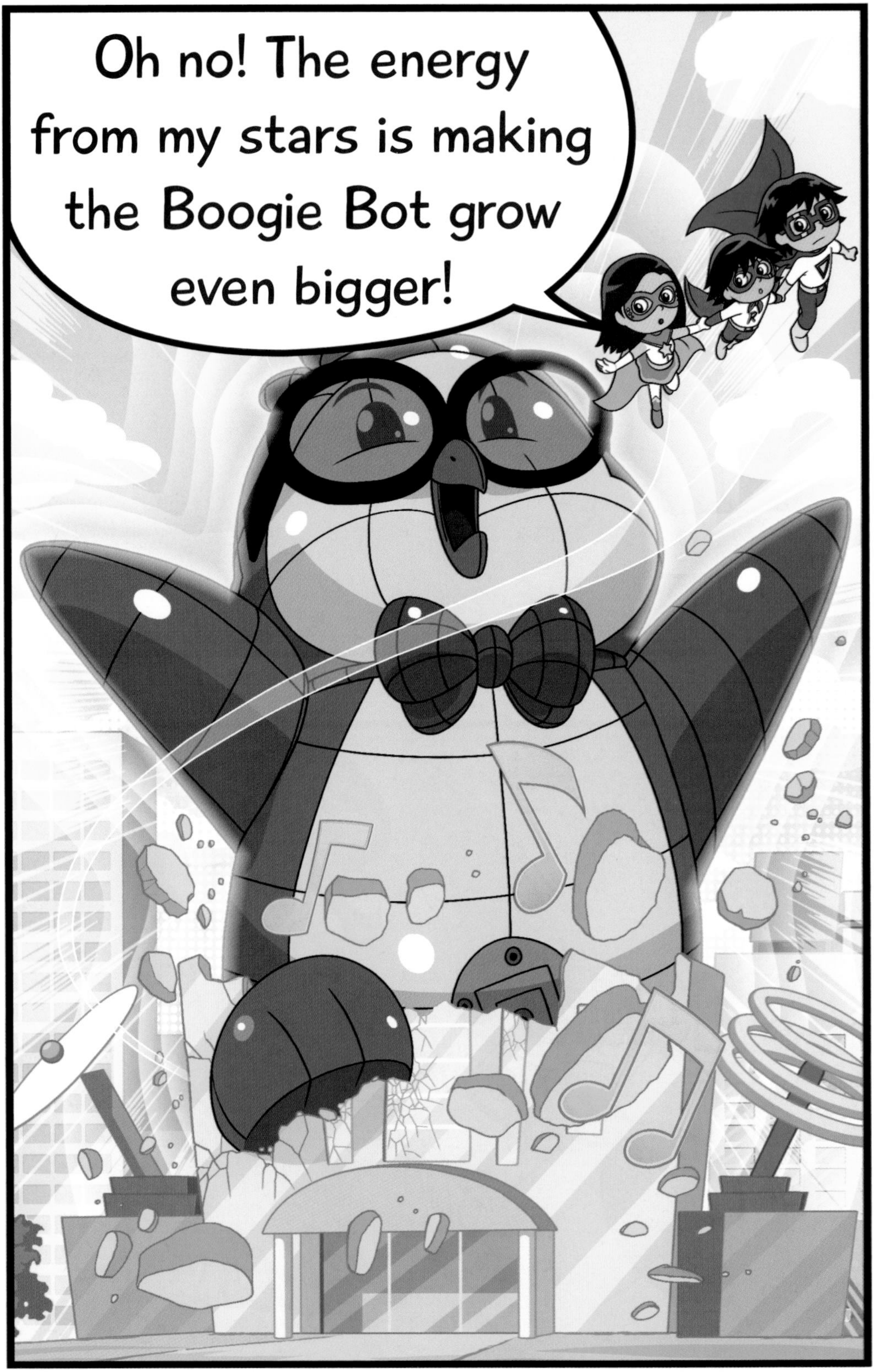
Oh no! The energy from my stars is making the Boogie Bot grow even bigger!

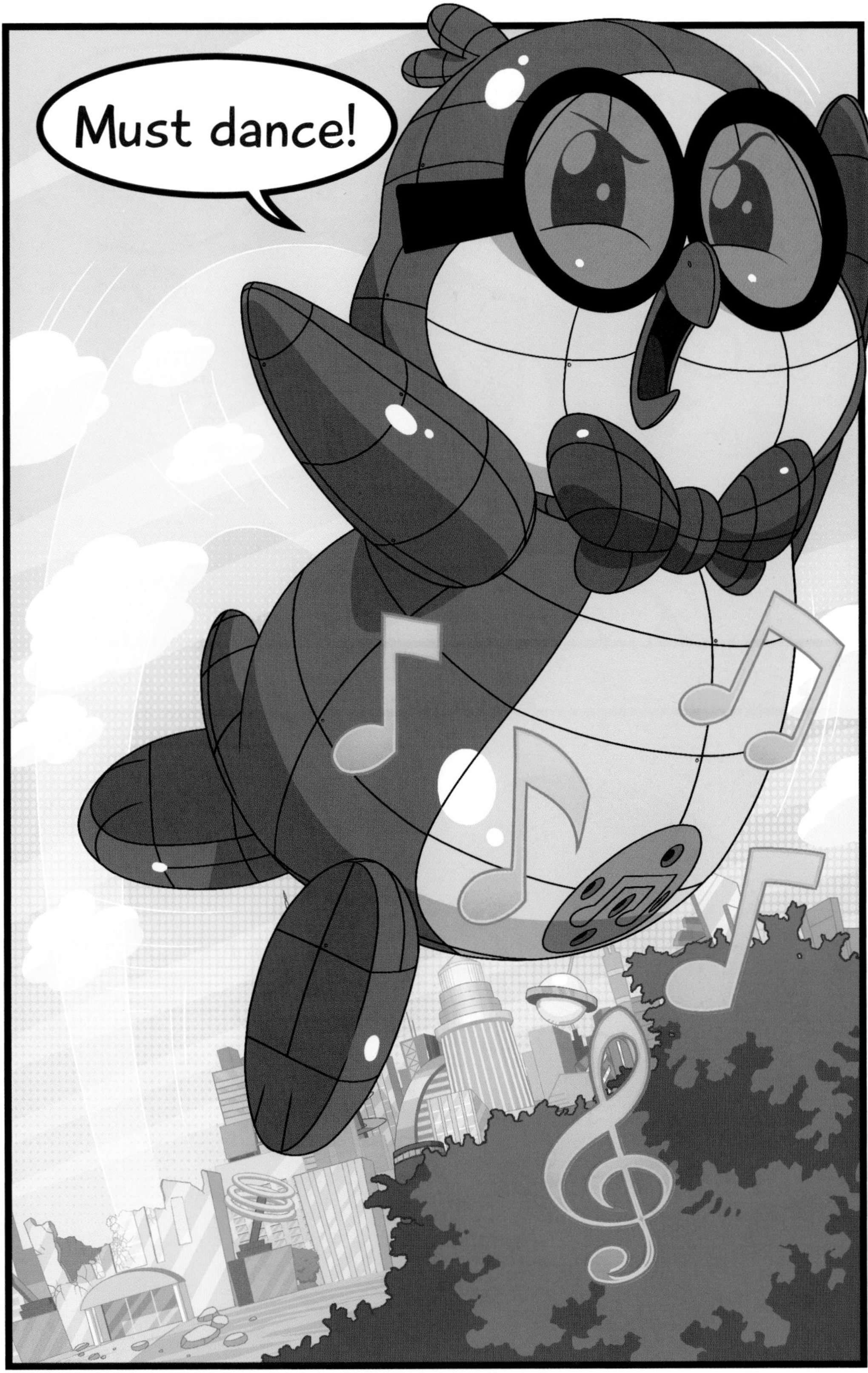
Must dance!

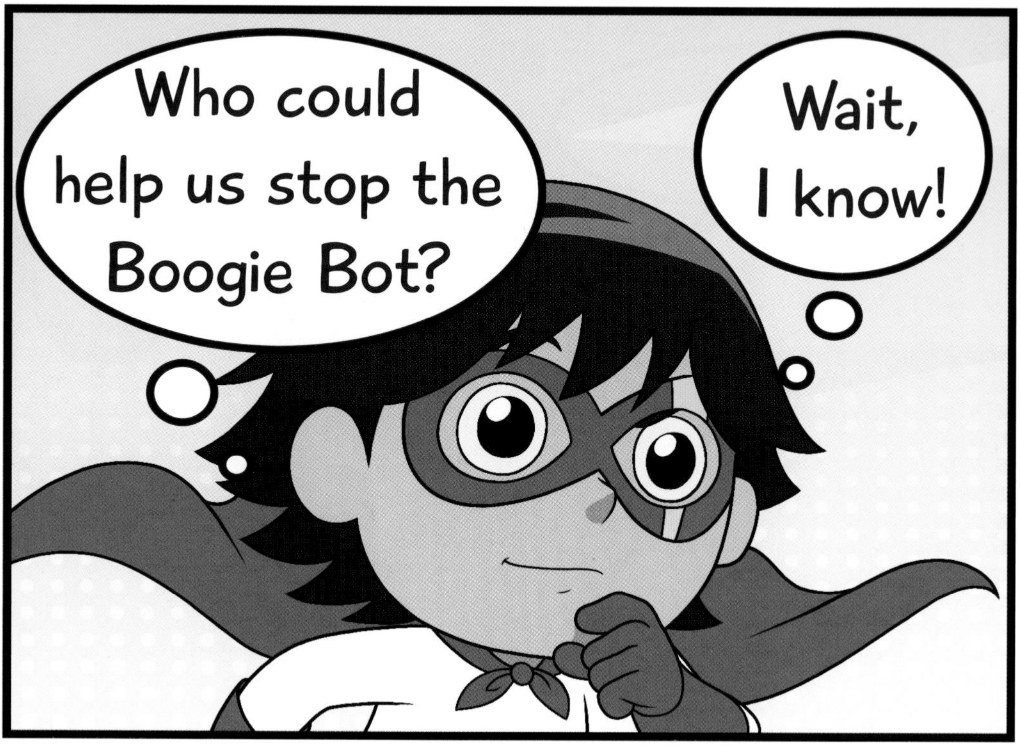
Who could help us stop the Boogie Bot?
Wait, I know!

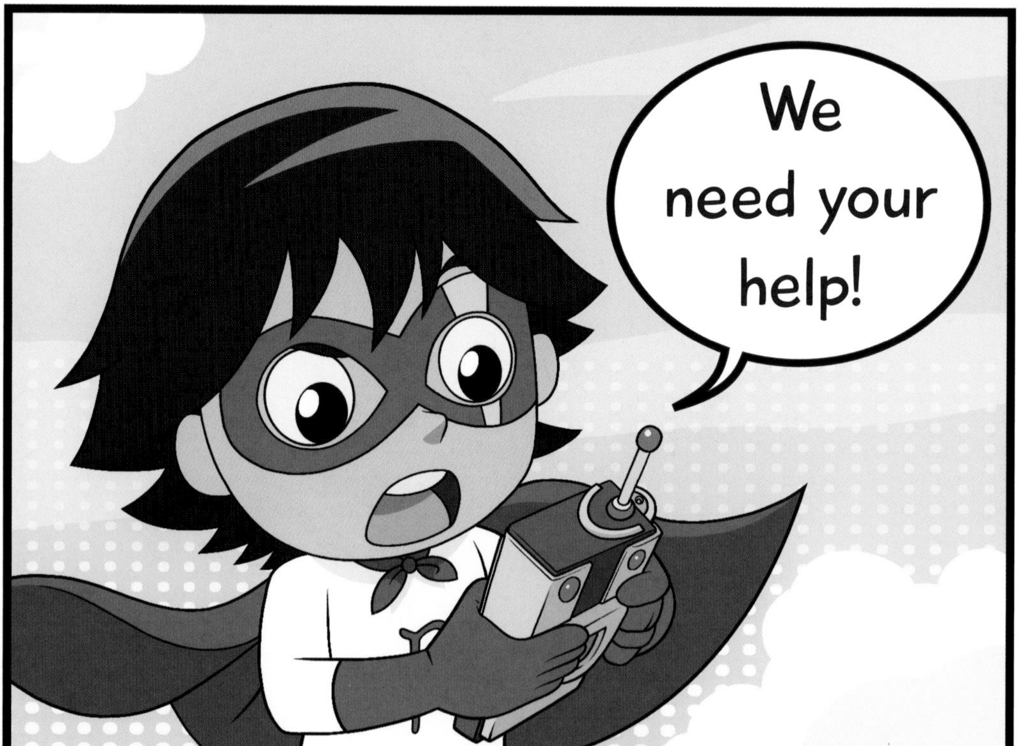
We need your help!

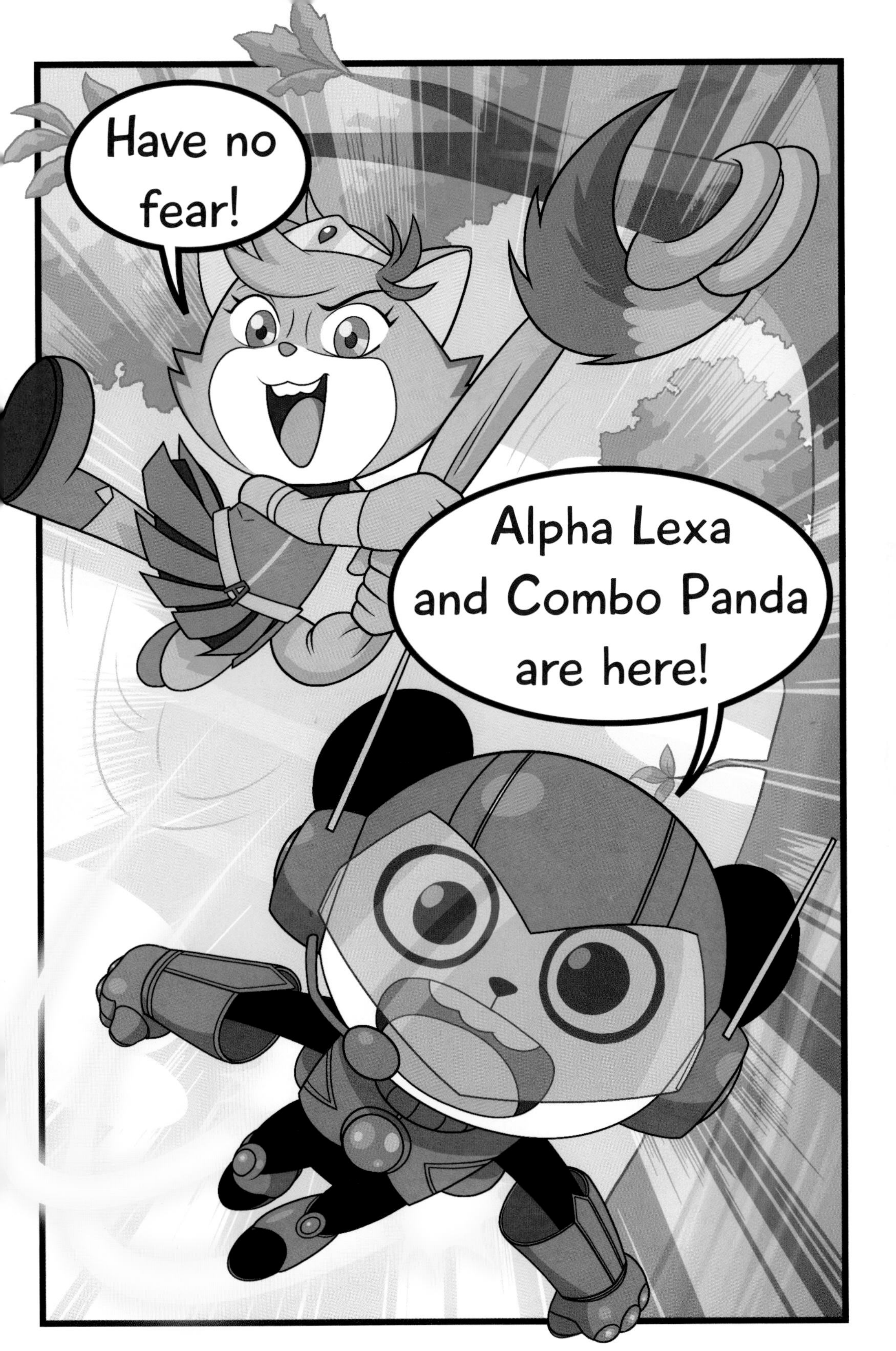
Have no fear!
Alpha Lexa and Combo Panda are here!

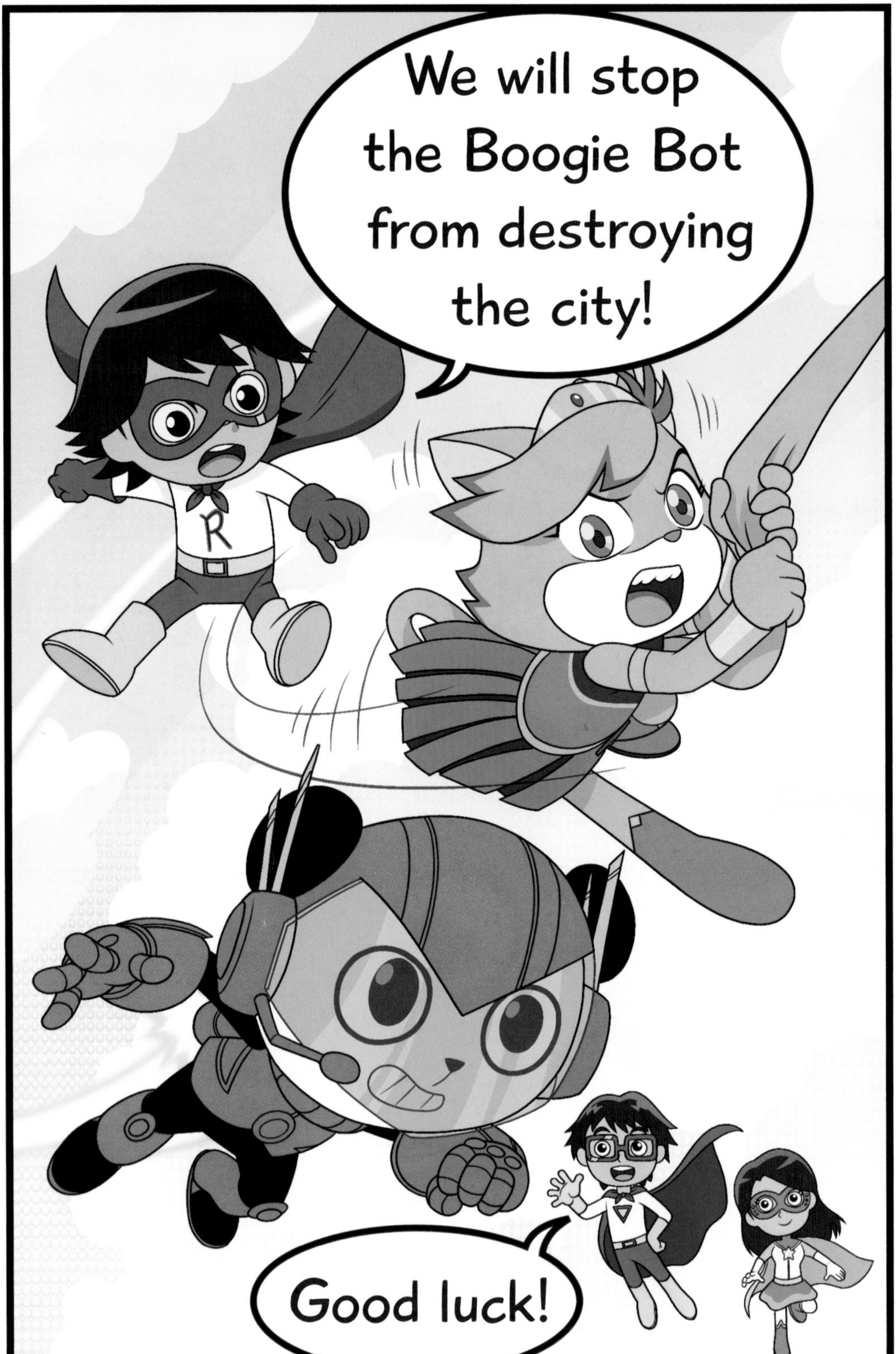
We will stop the Boogie Bot from destroying the city!
Good luck!

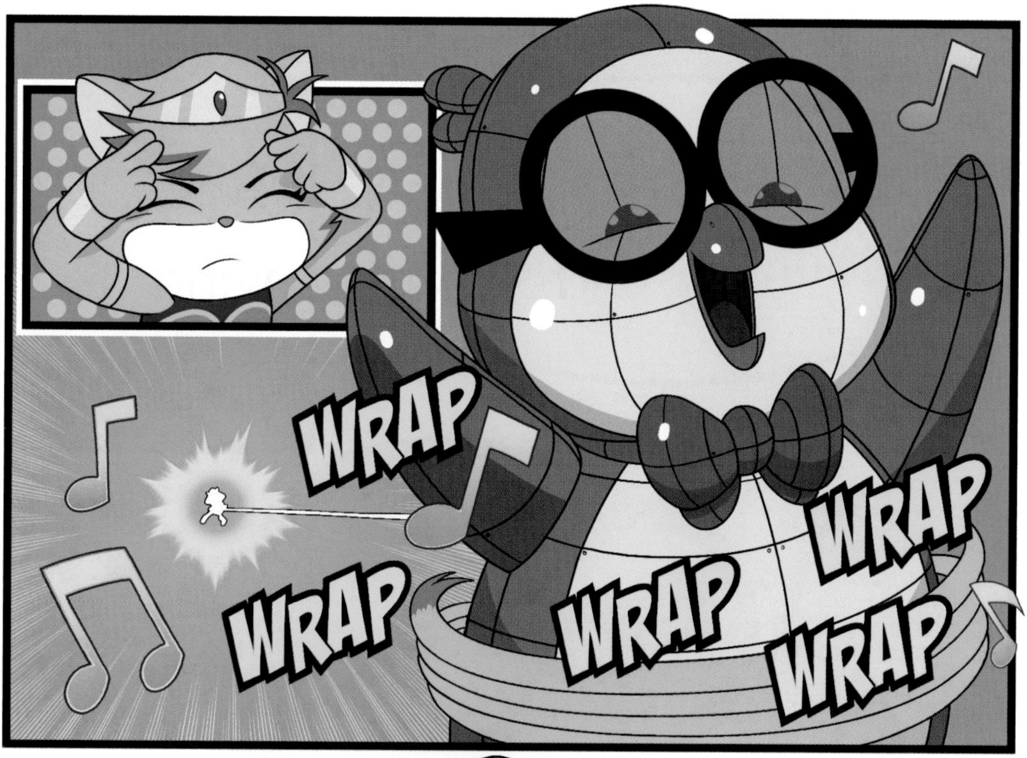
WRAP
WRAP
WRAP
WRAP
WRAP

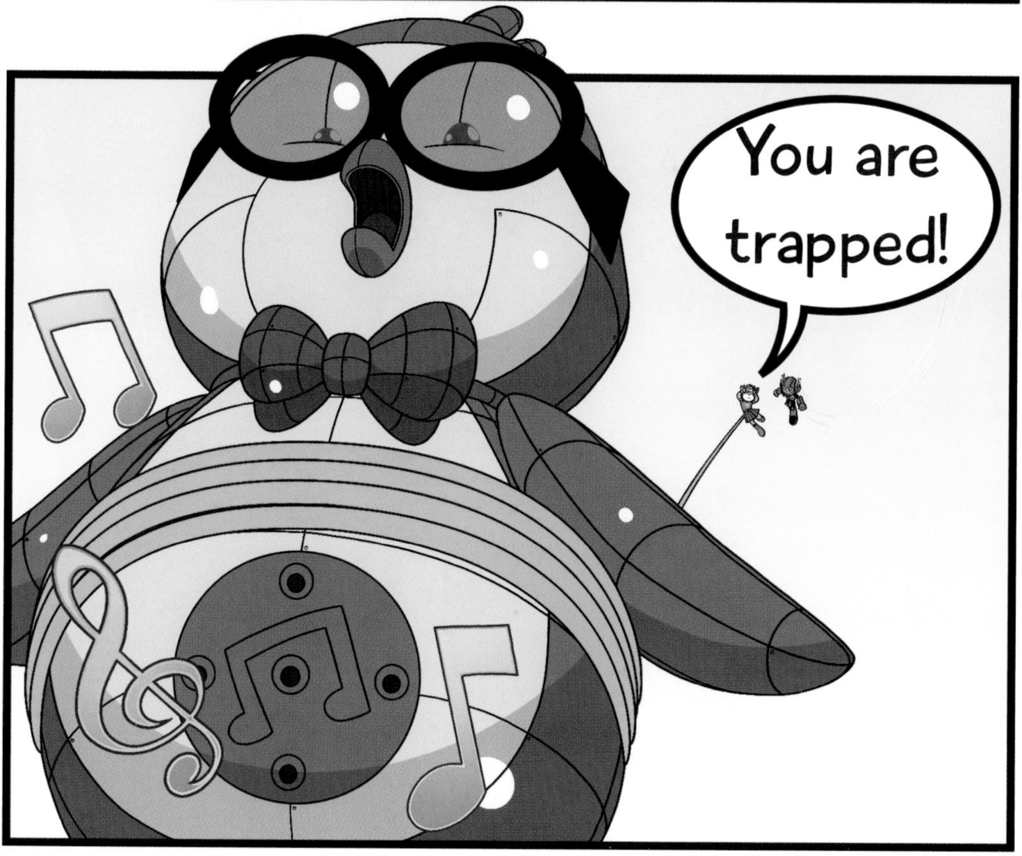
You are trapped!

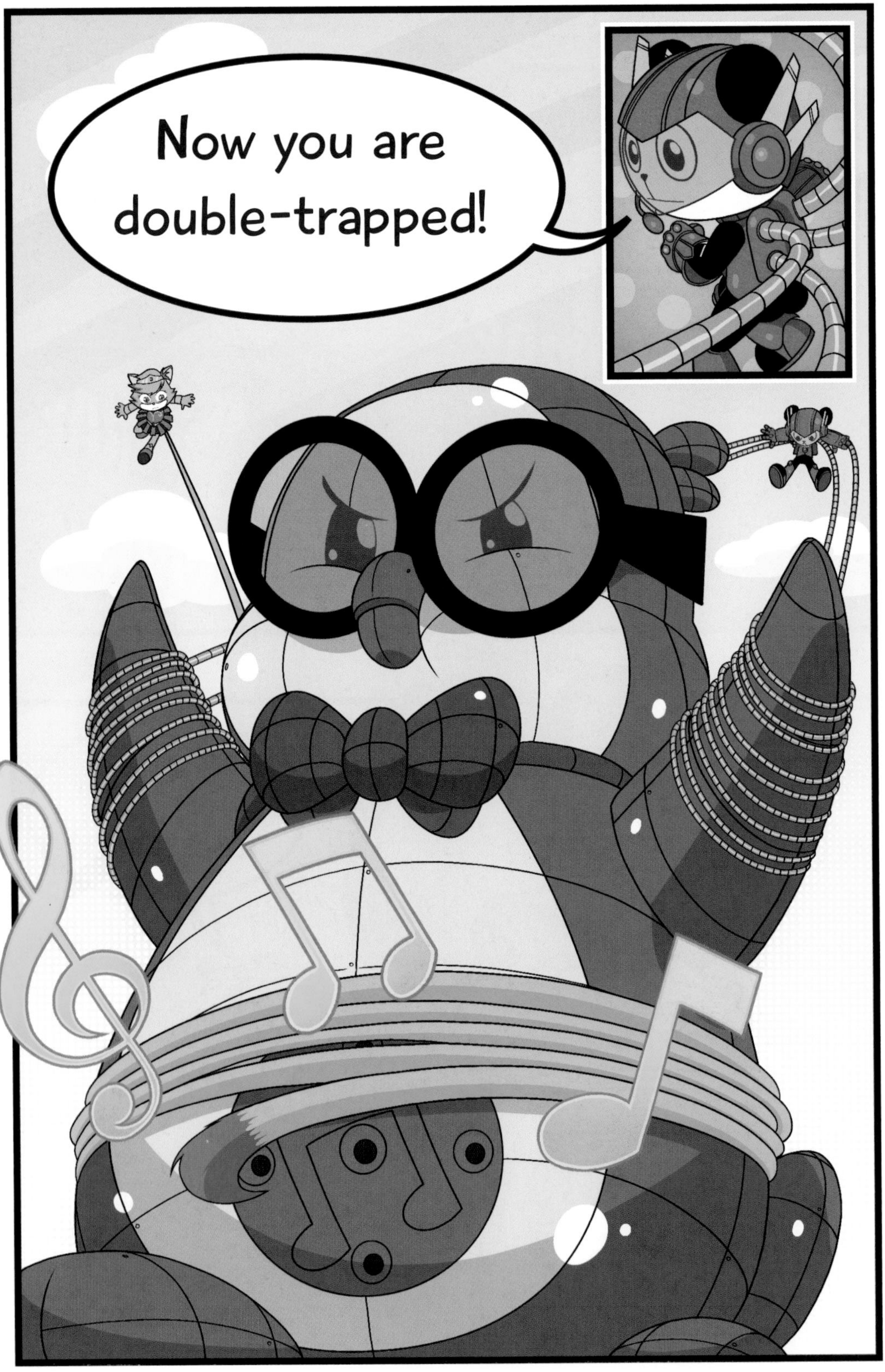
Now you are double-trapped!

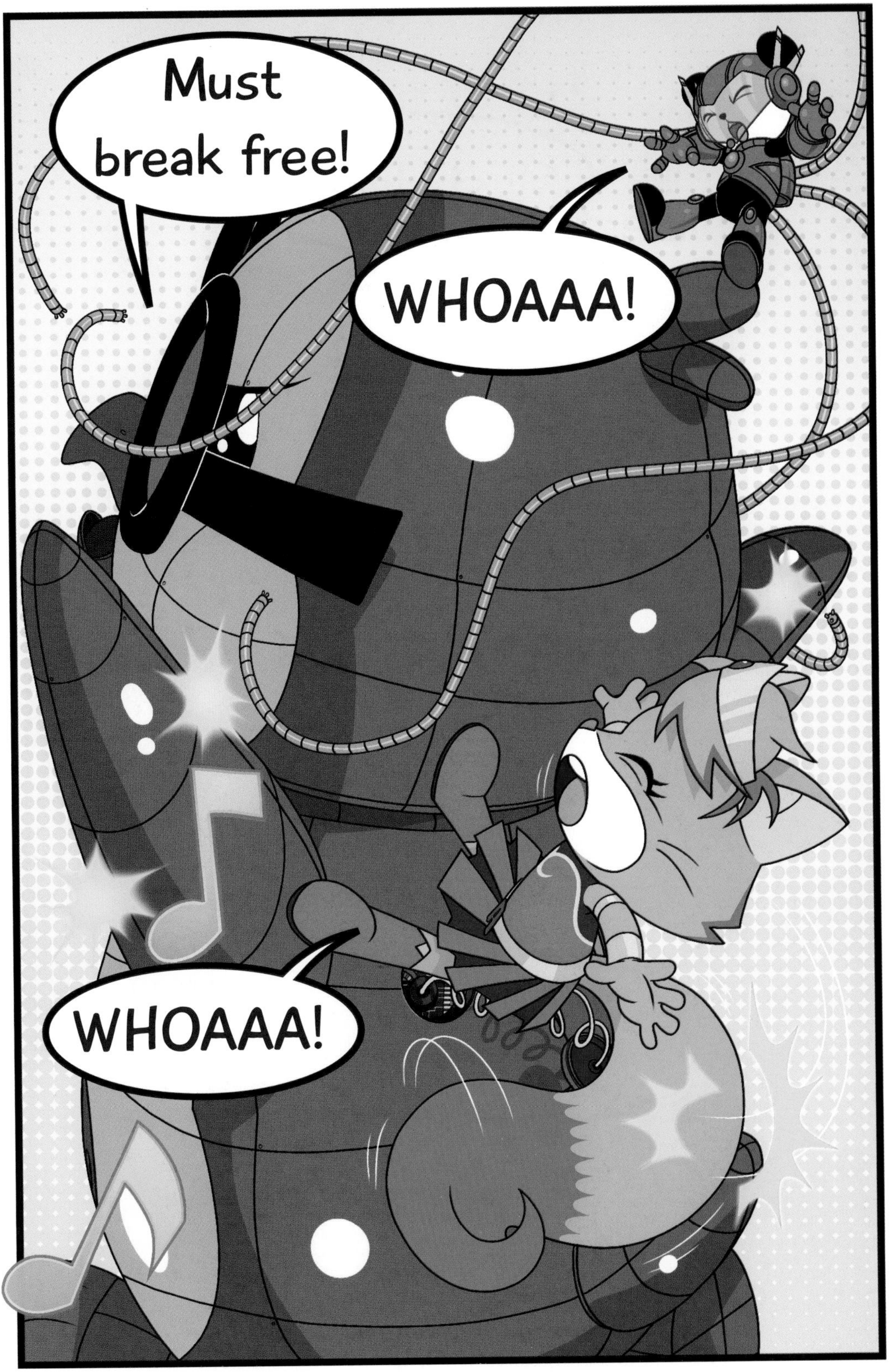
Must break free!
WHOAAA!
WHOAAA!

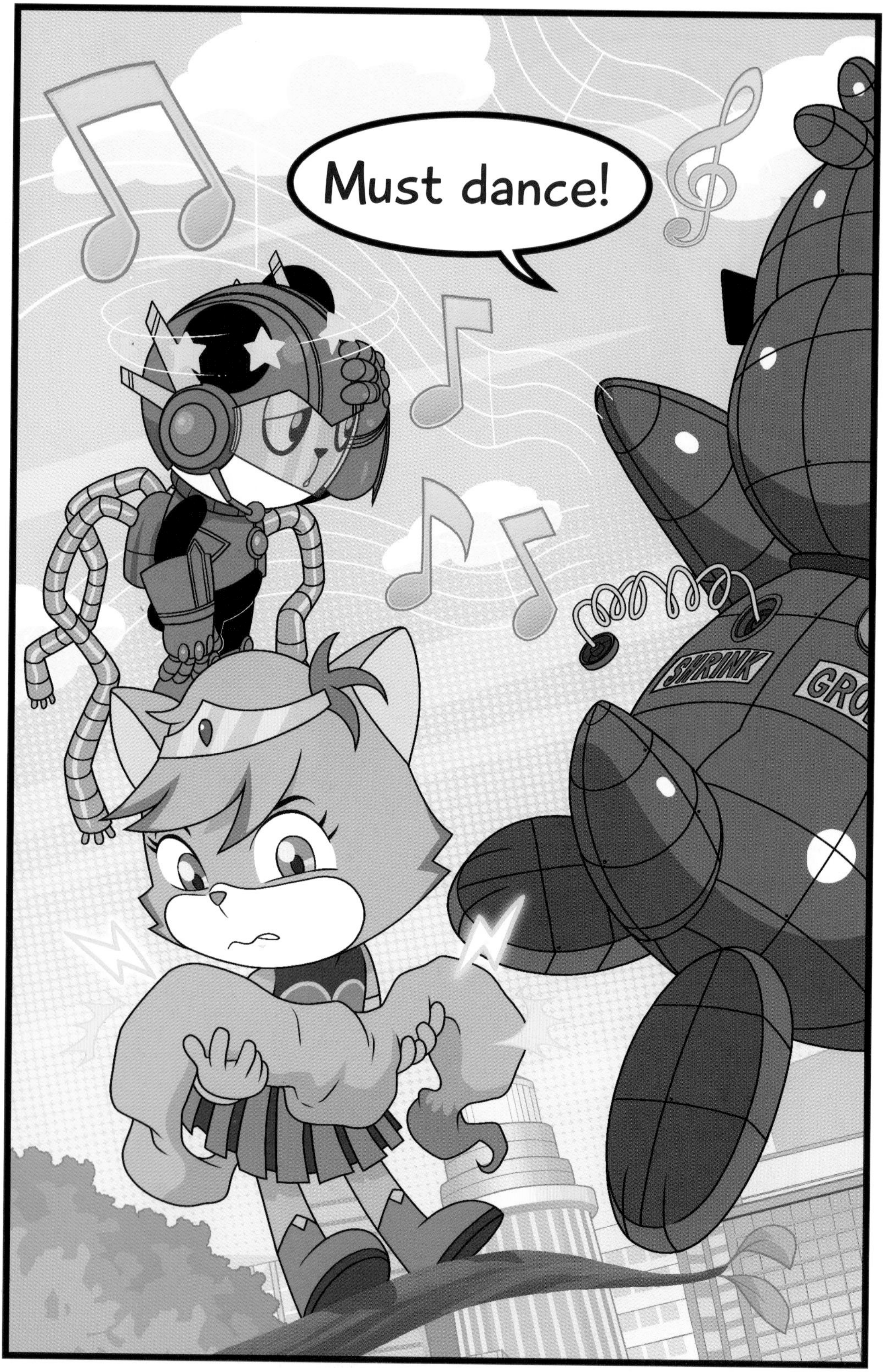
Must dance!
SHRINK

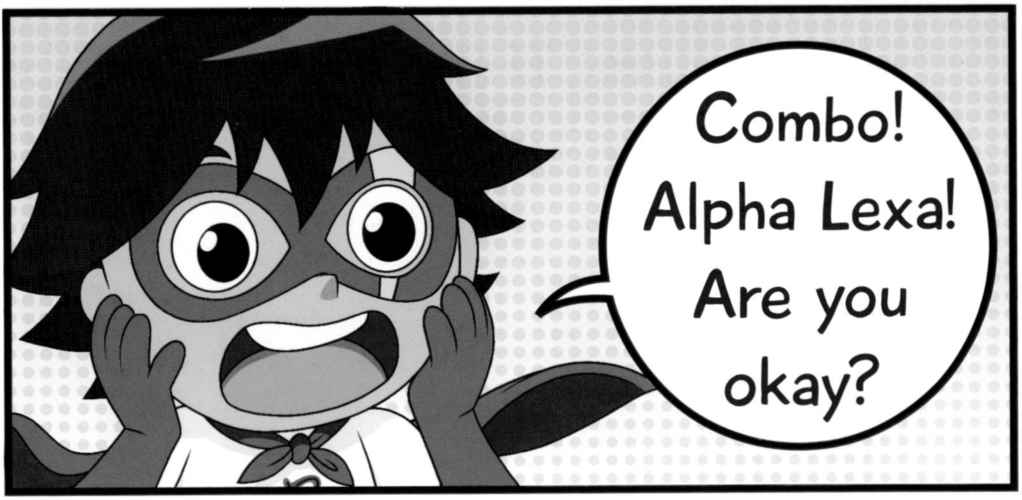
Combo! Alpha Lexa! Are you okay?

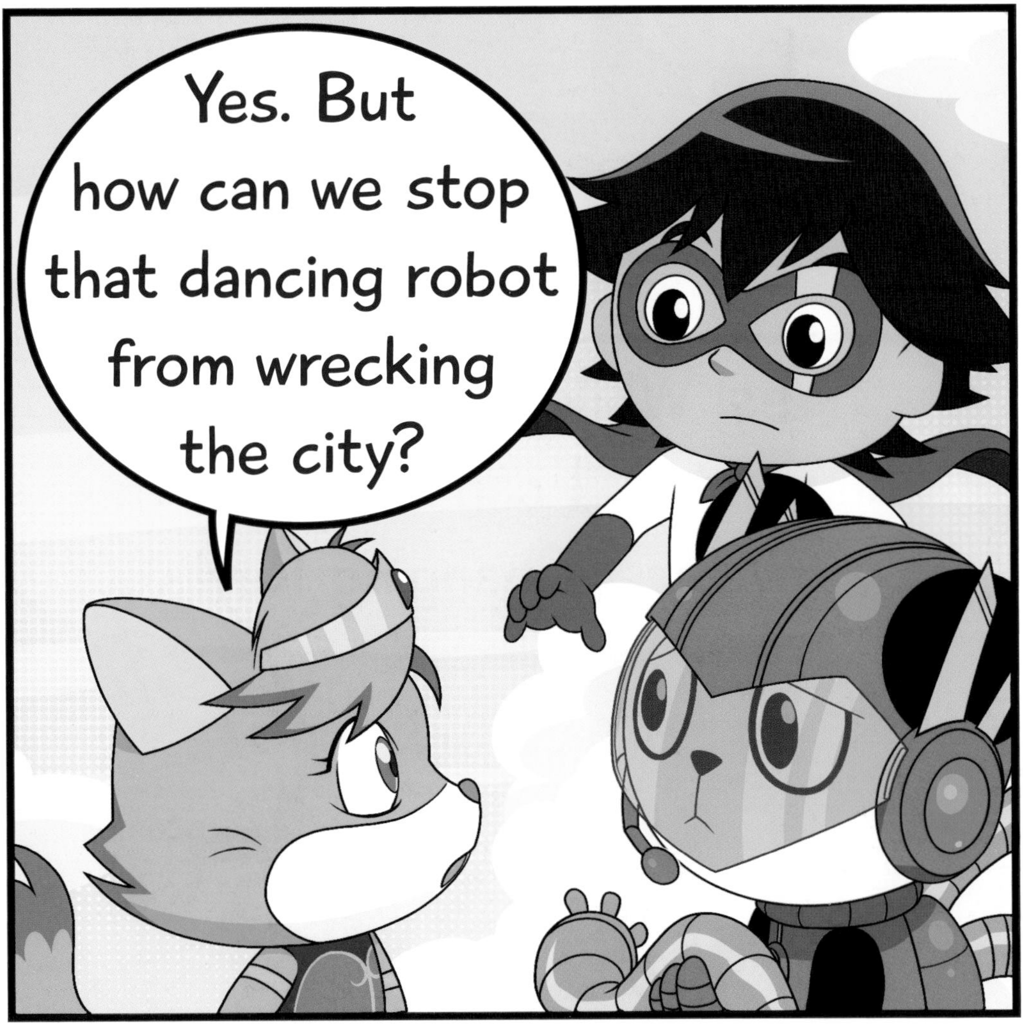
Yes. But how can we stop that dancing robot from wrecking the city?

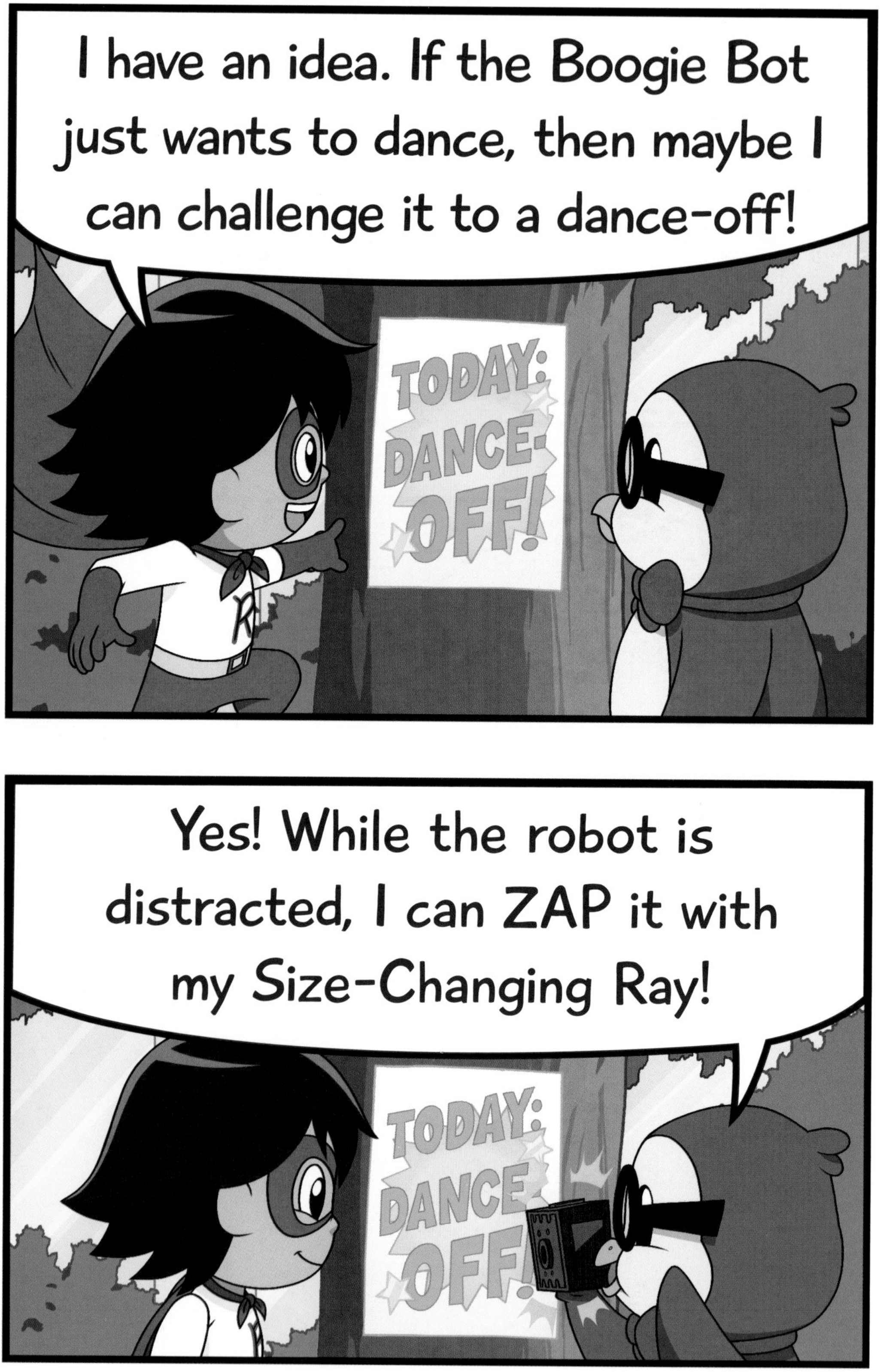
I have an idea. If the Boogie Bot just wants to dance, then maybe I can challenge it to a dance-off!
TODAY: DANCE-OFF!
Yes! While the robot is distracted, I can ZAP it with my Size-Changing Ray!
TODAY: DANCE-OFF!

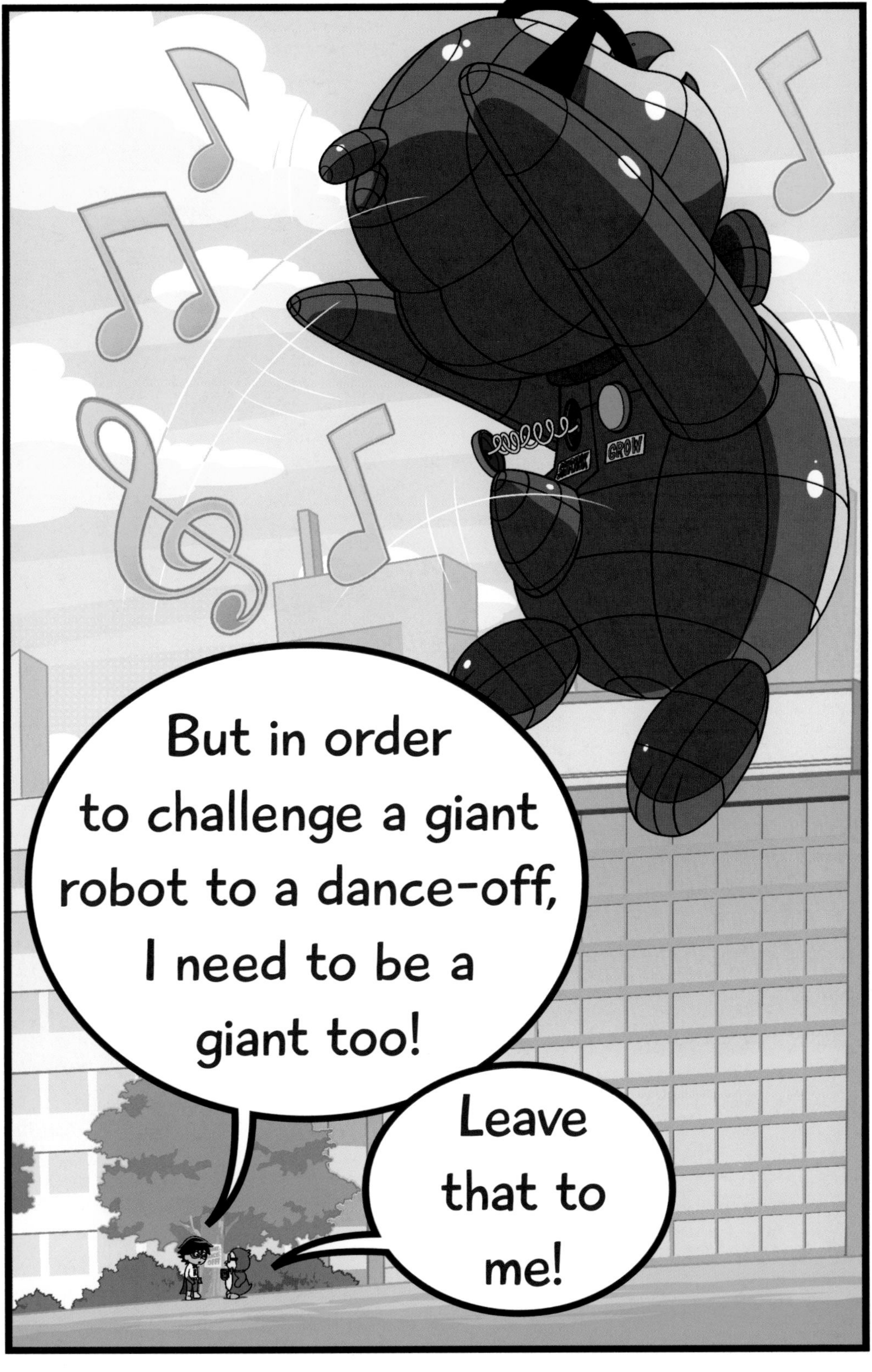
GROW
But in order to challenge a giant robot to a dance-off, I need to be a giant too!
Leave that to me!

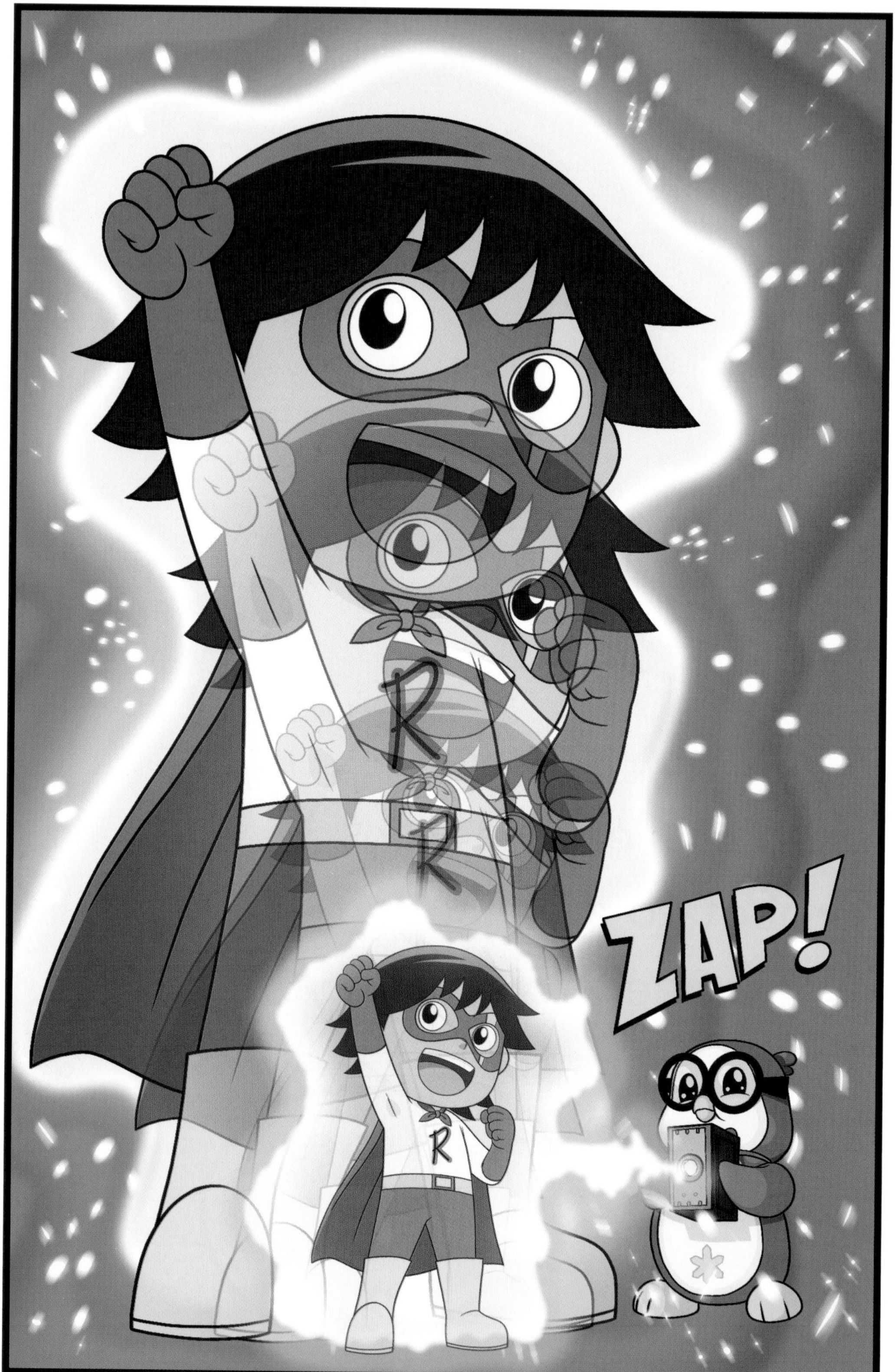
ZAP!

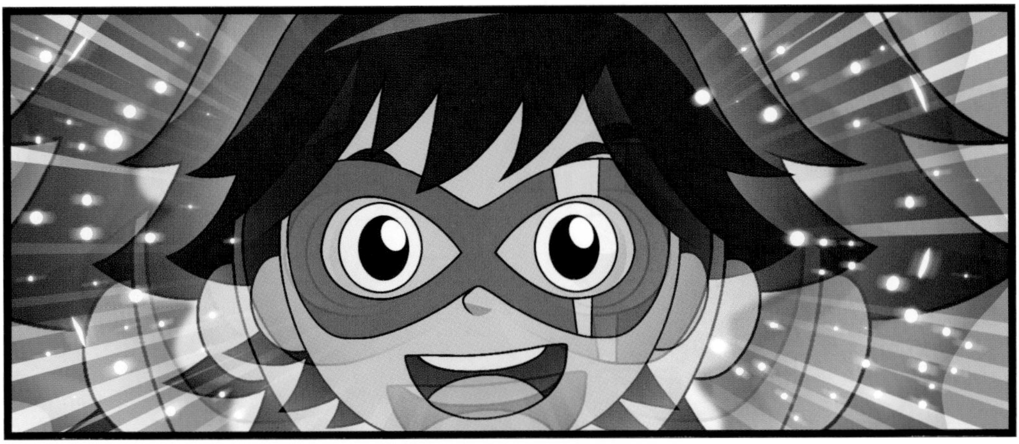

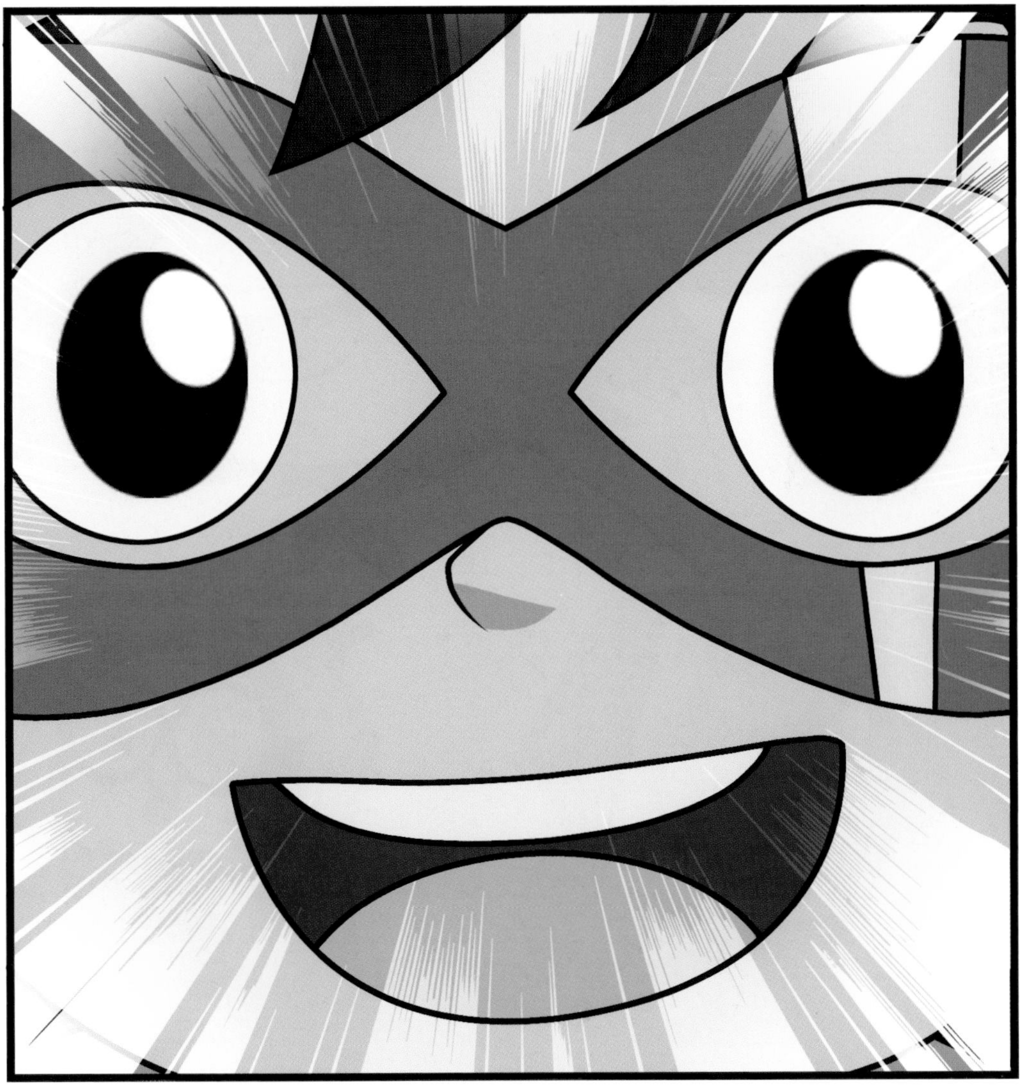

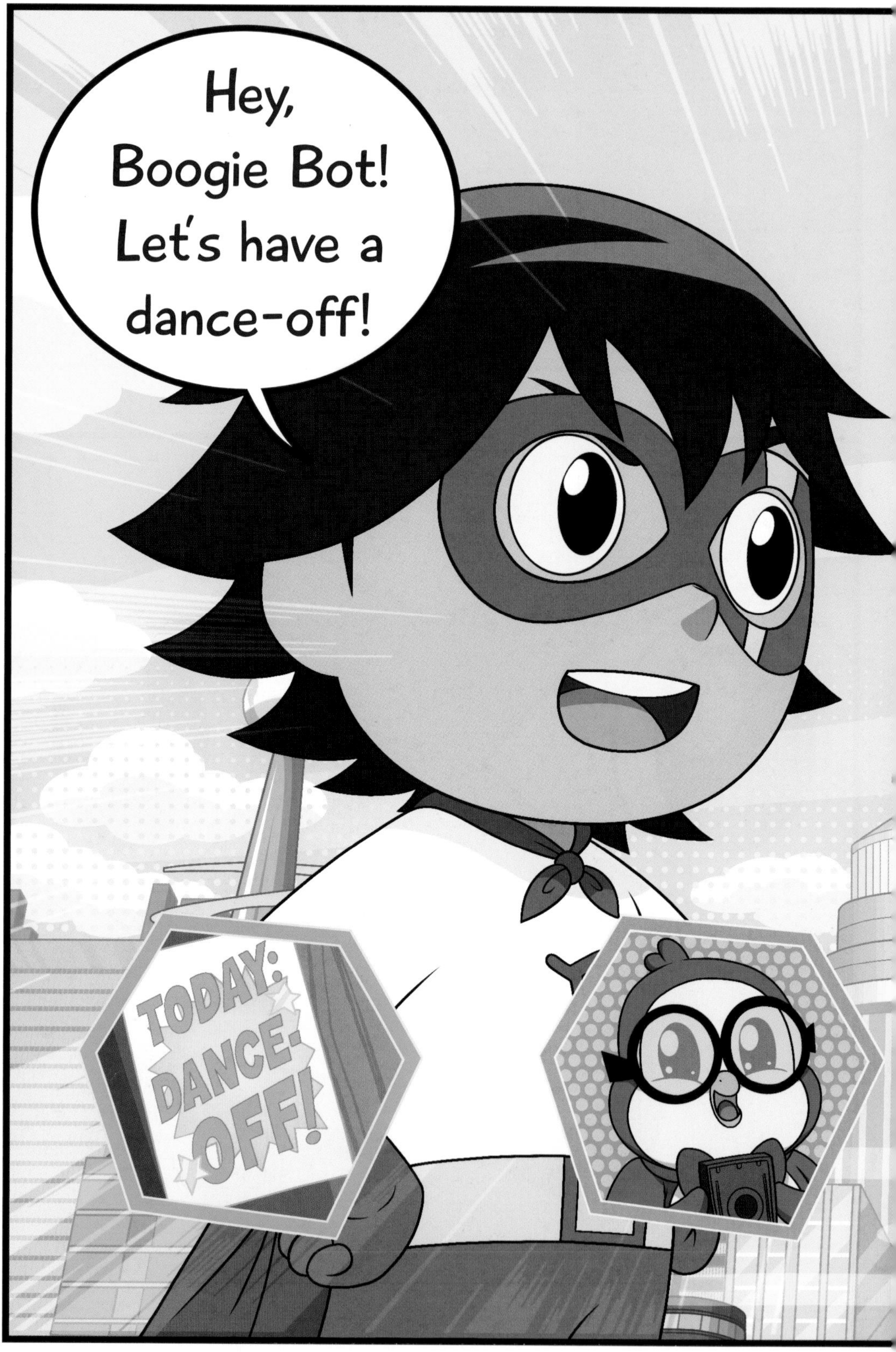
Hey,
Boogie Bot!
Let's have a
dance-off!
TODAY:
DANCE-
OFF!

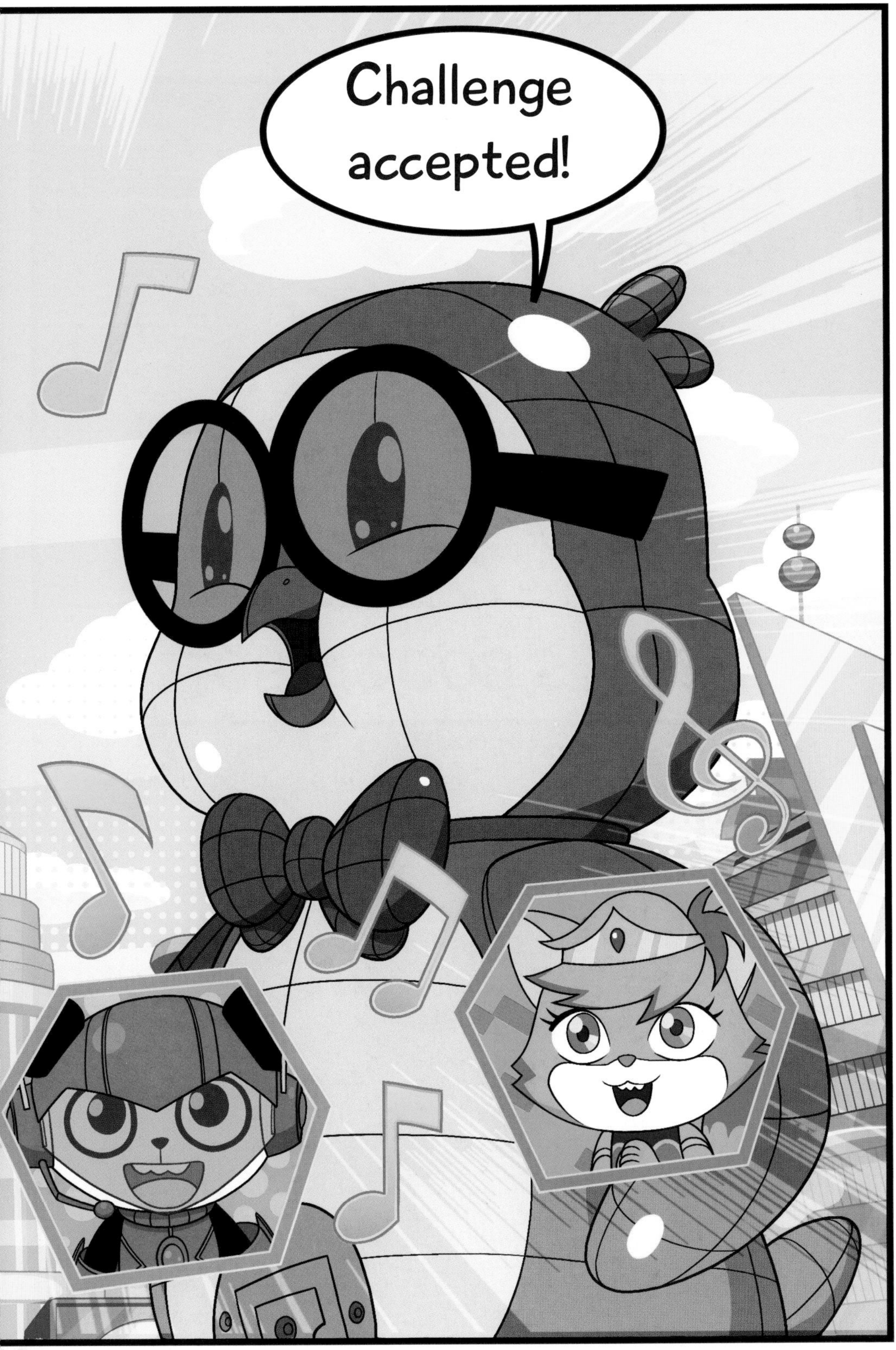
Challenge accepted!

RED TITAN

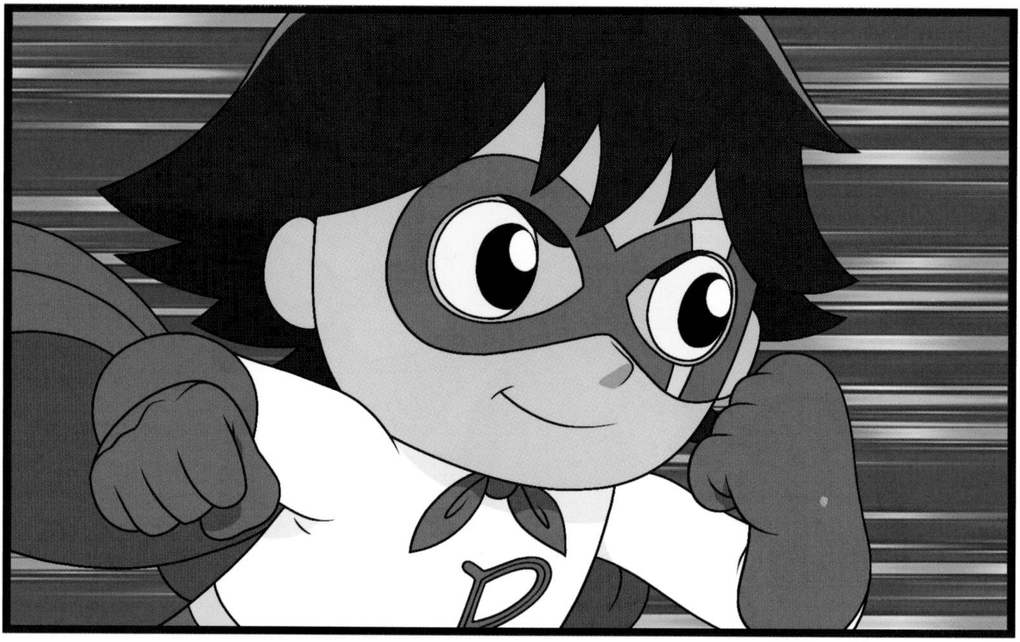

VERSUS BOOGIE BOT

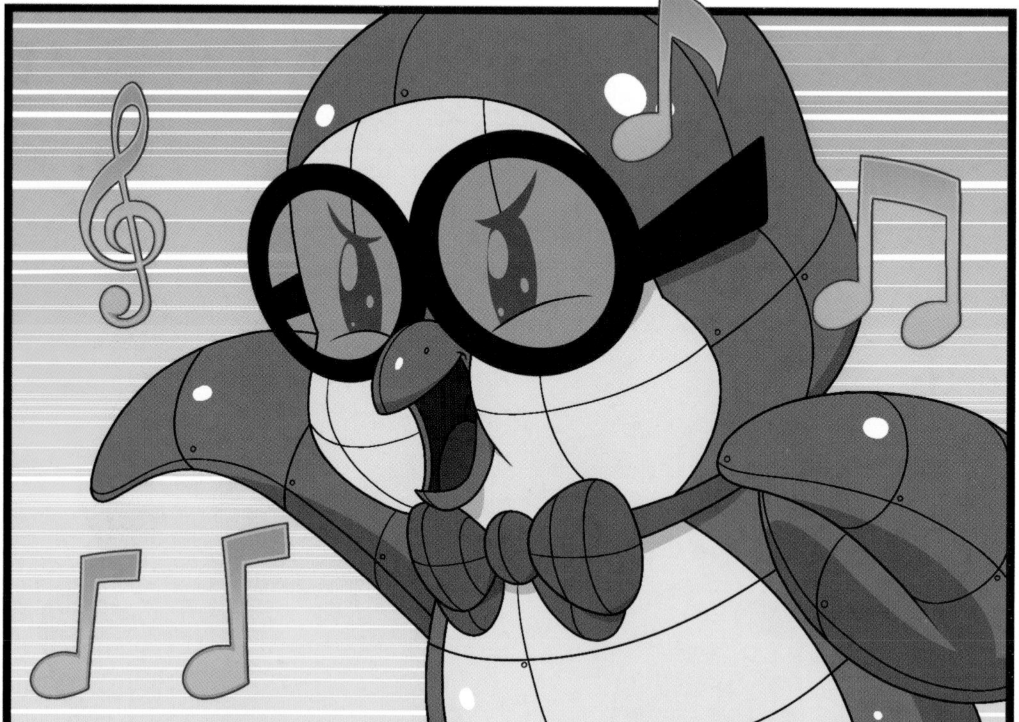

# BEGIN!

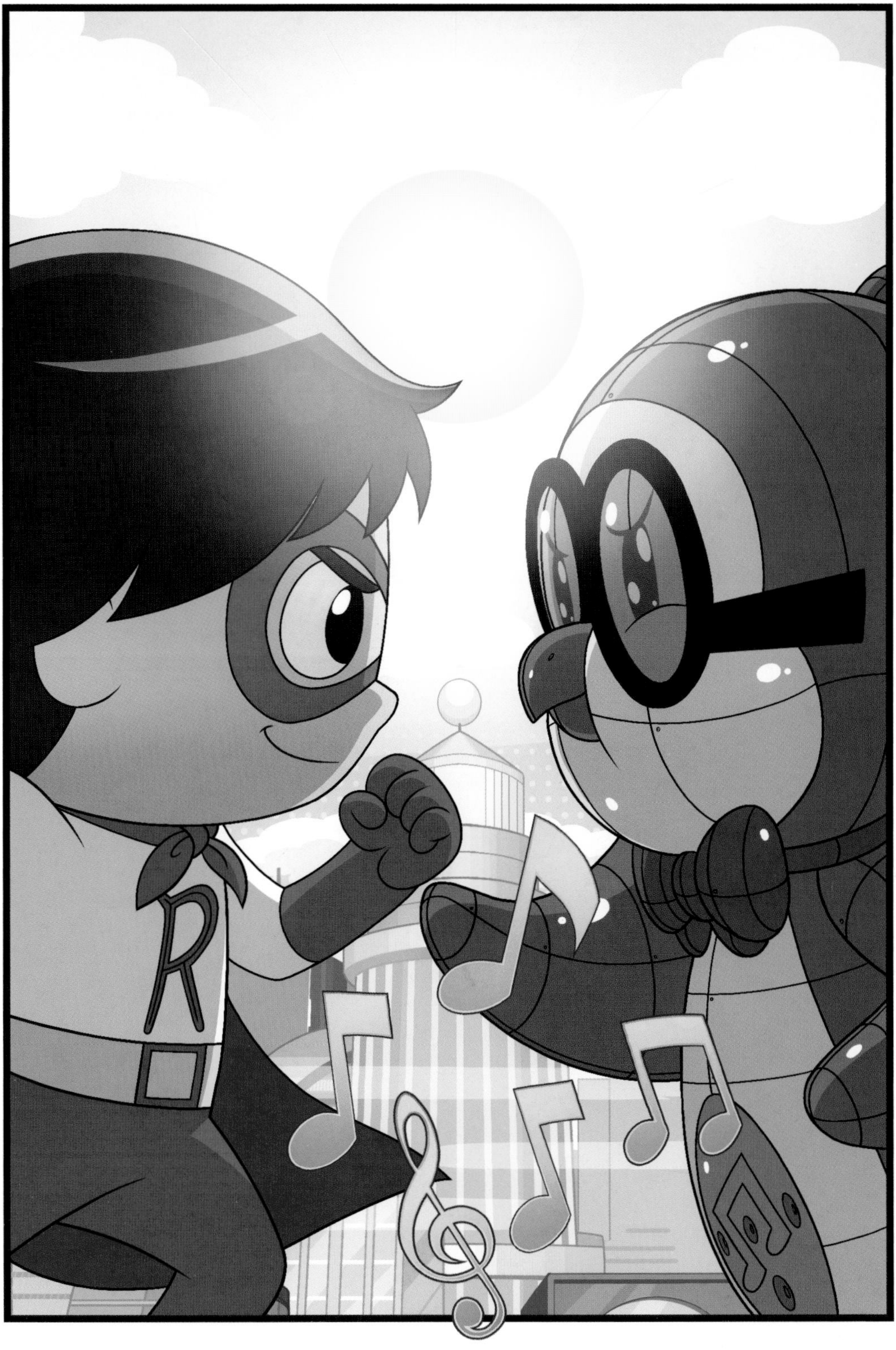

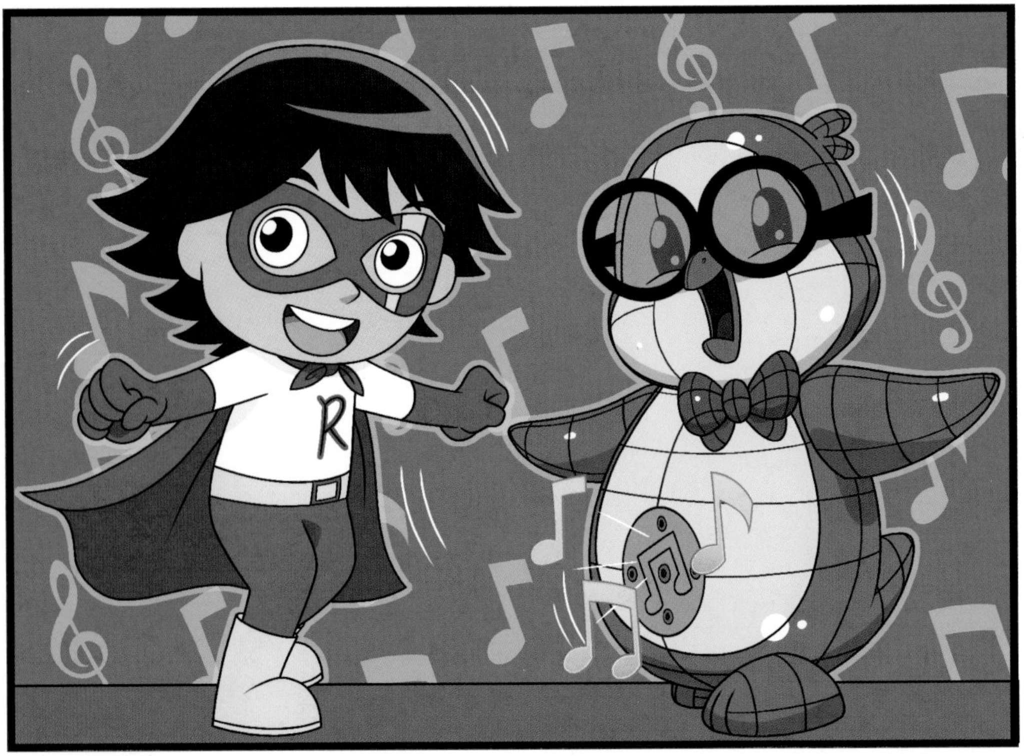

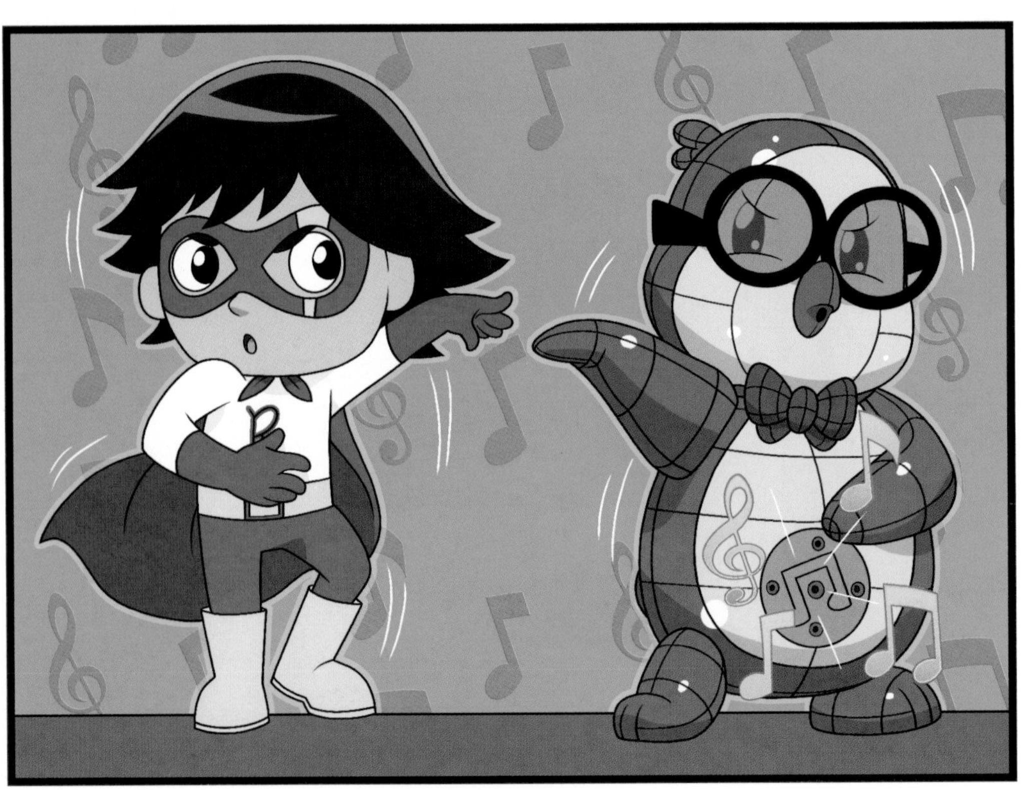

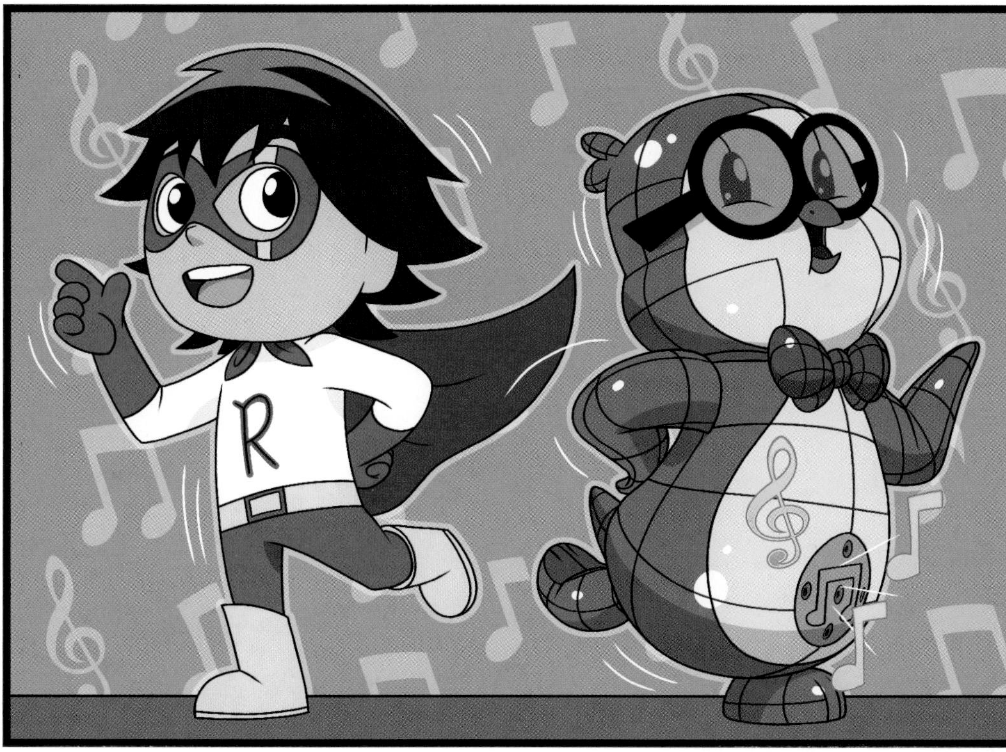
R

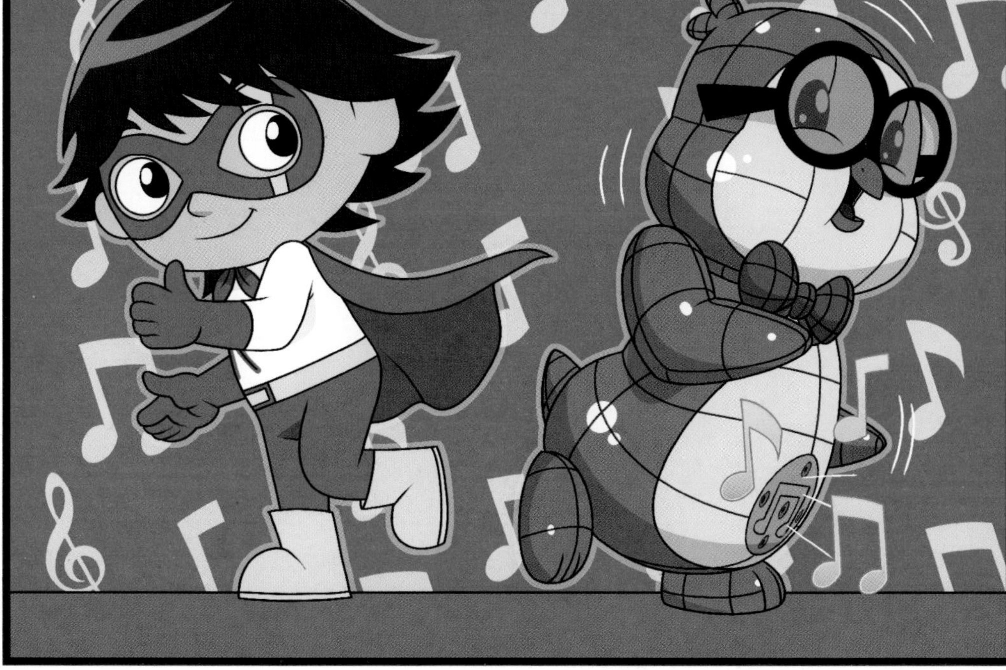

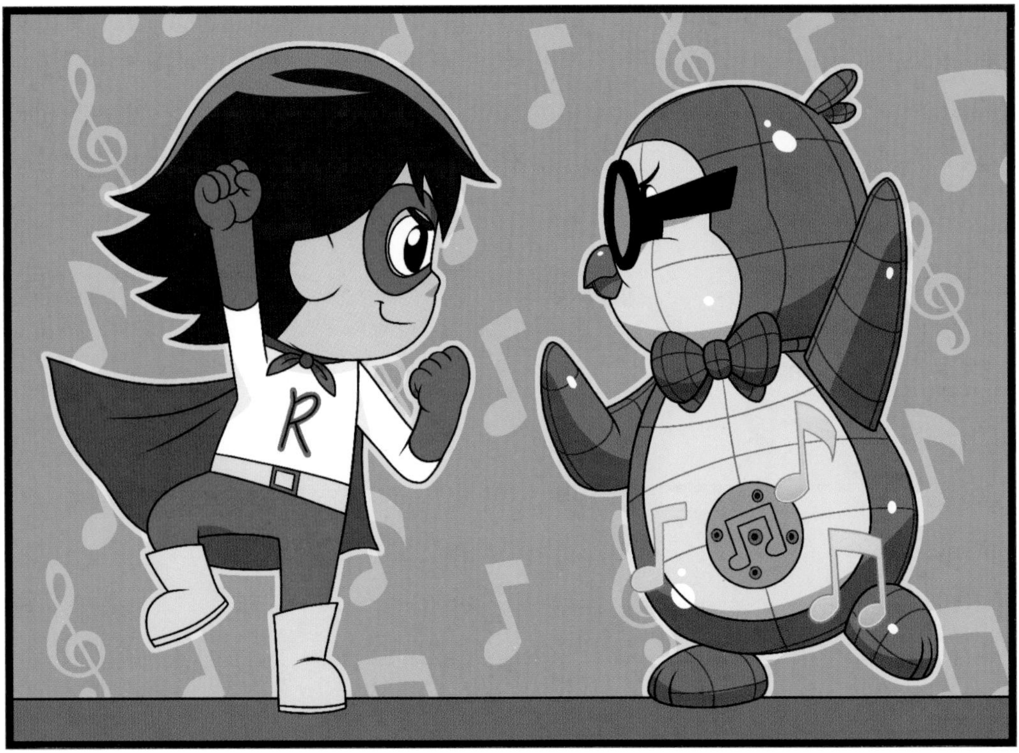

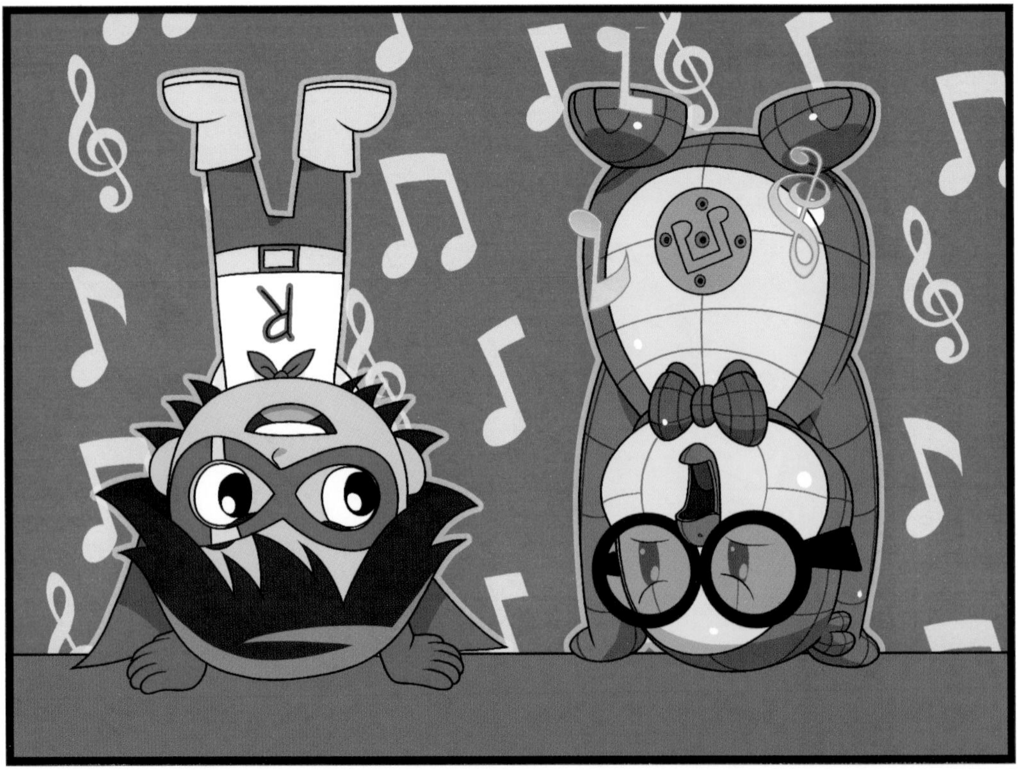

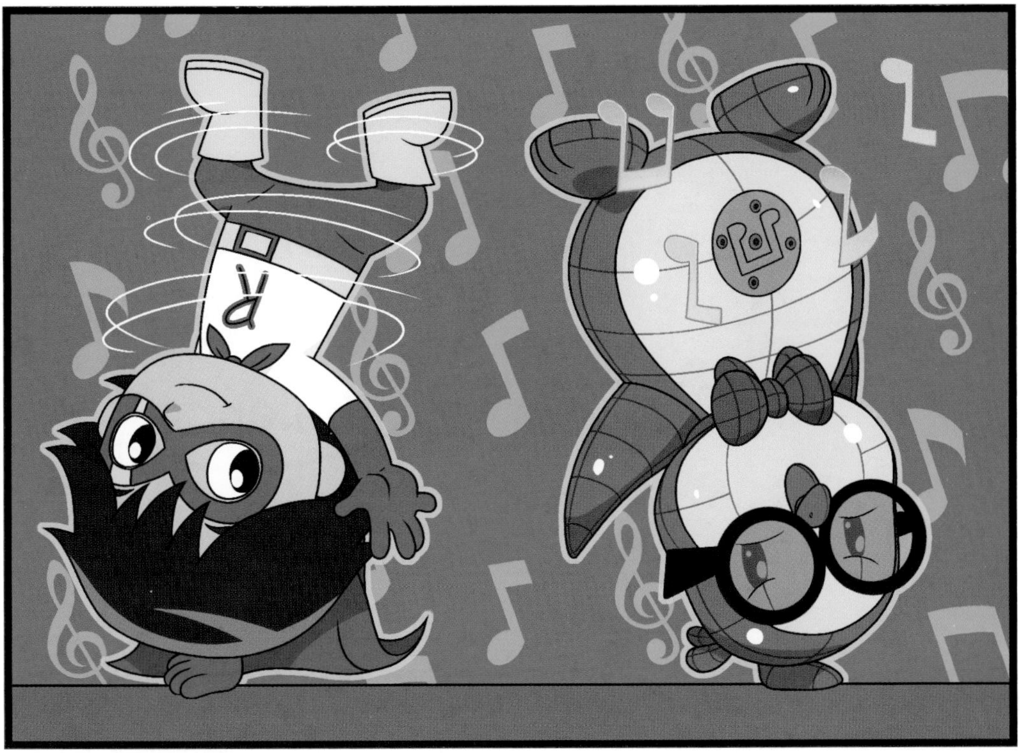

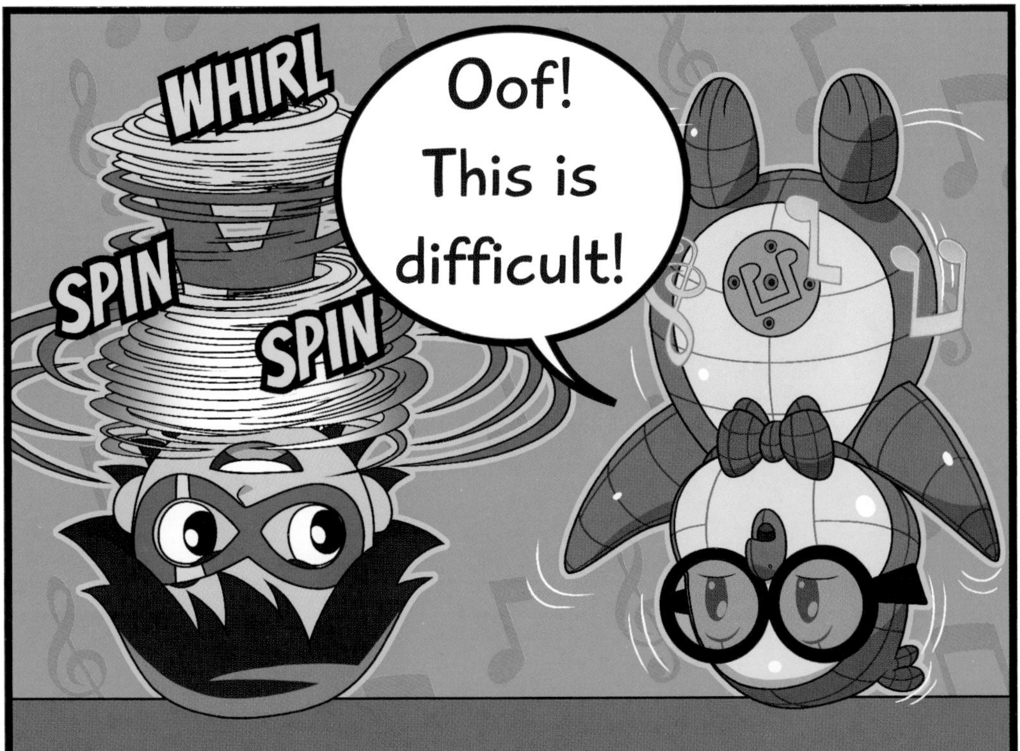
WHIRL
SPIN
SPIN
Oof! This is difficult!

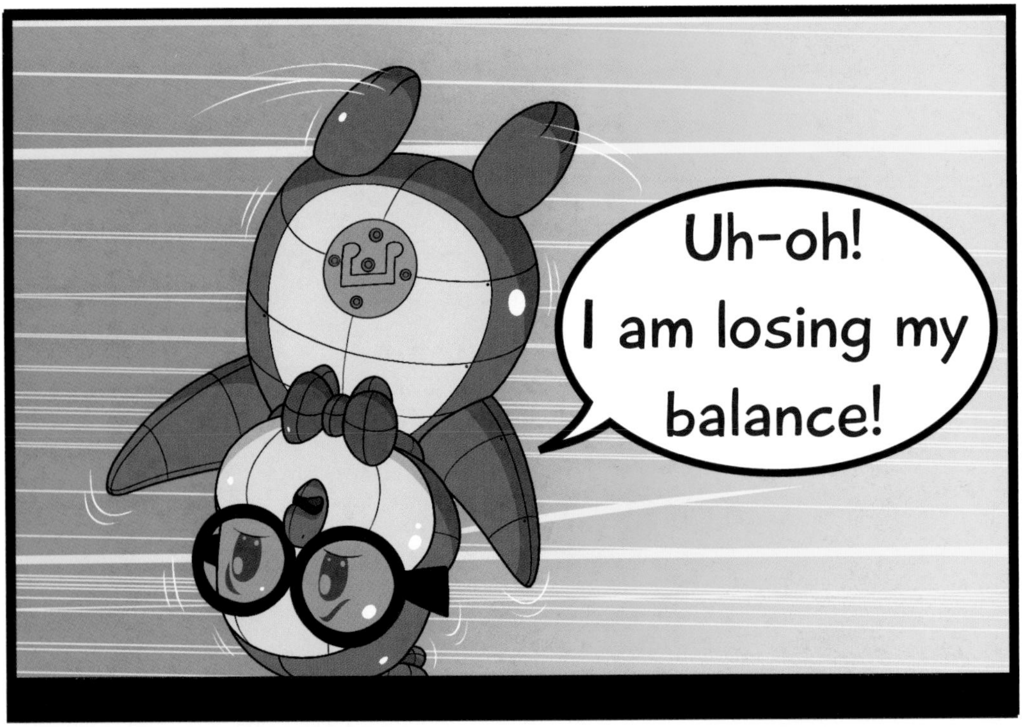
Uh-oh!
I am losing my
balance!

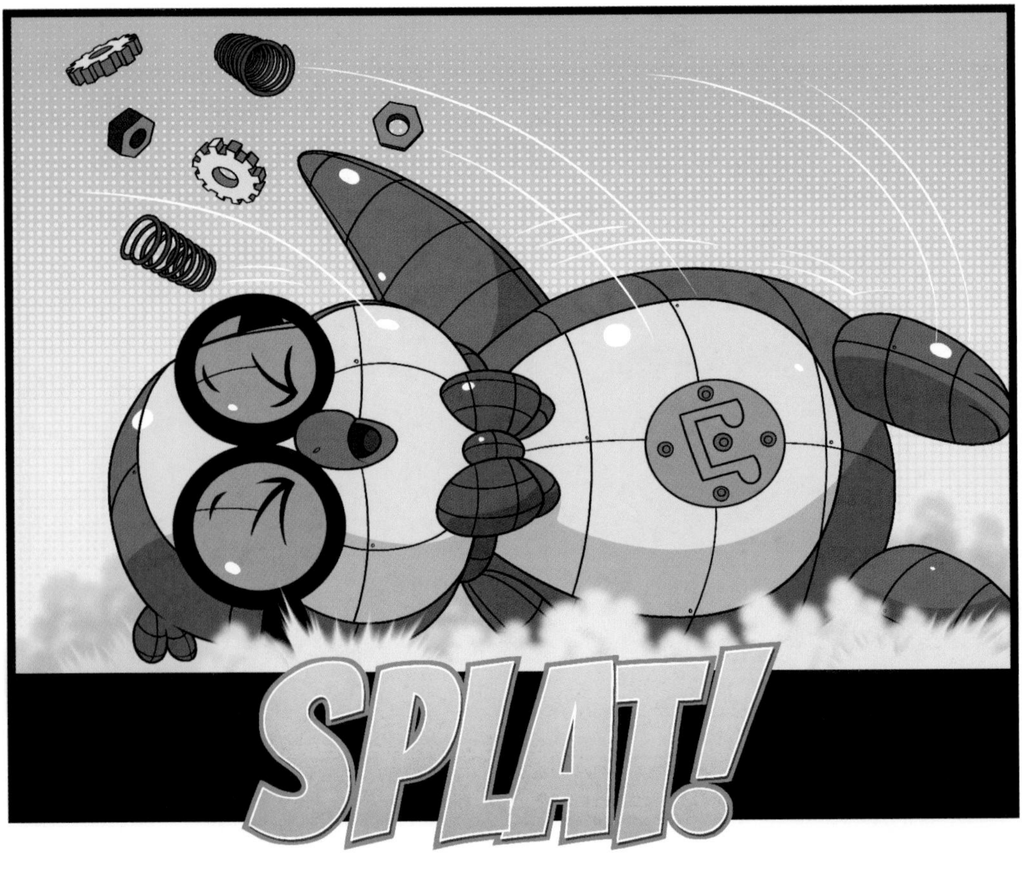
SPLAT!

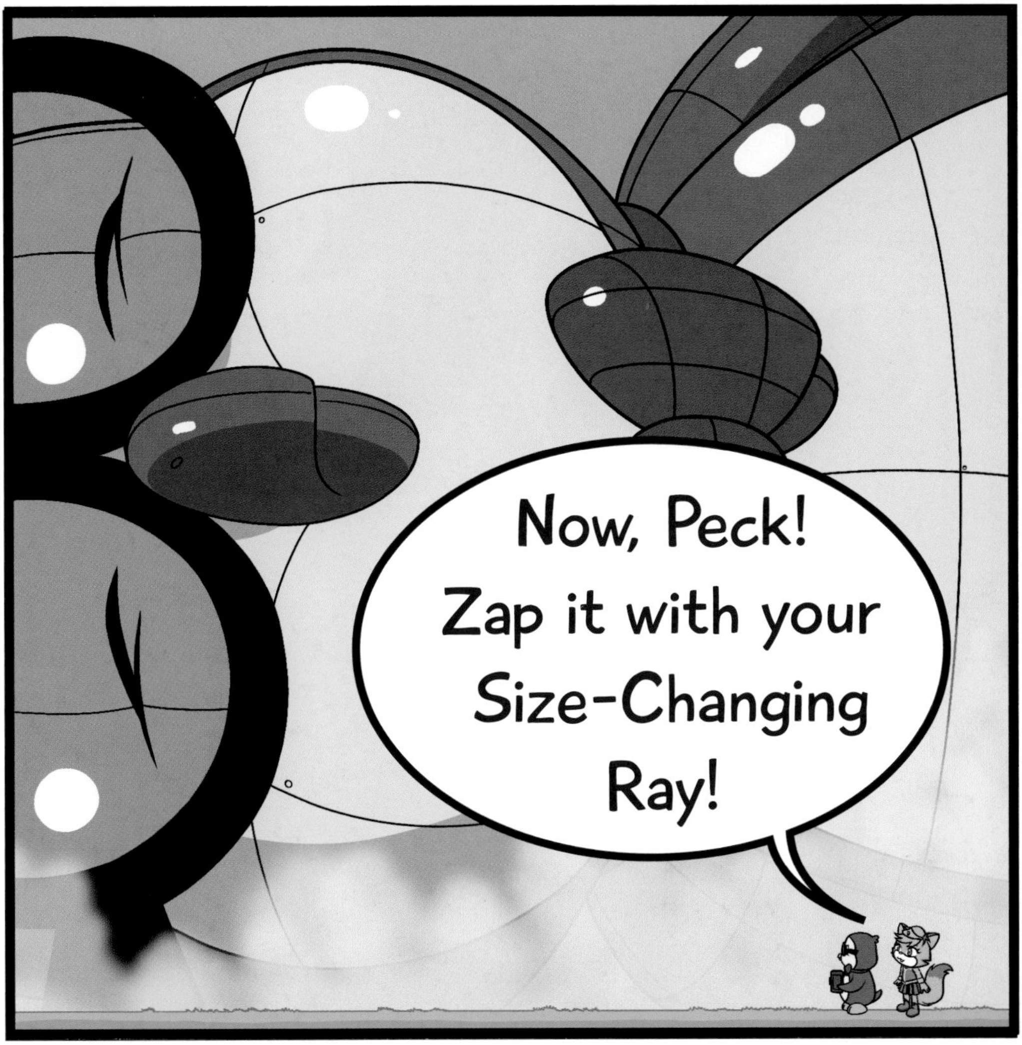
Now, Peck! Zap it with your Size-Changing Ray!

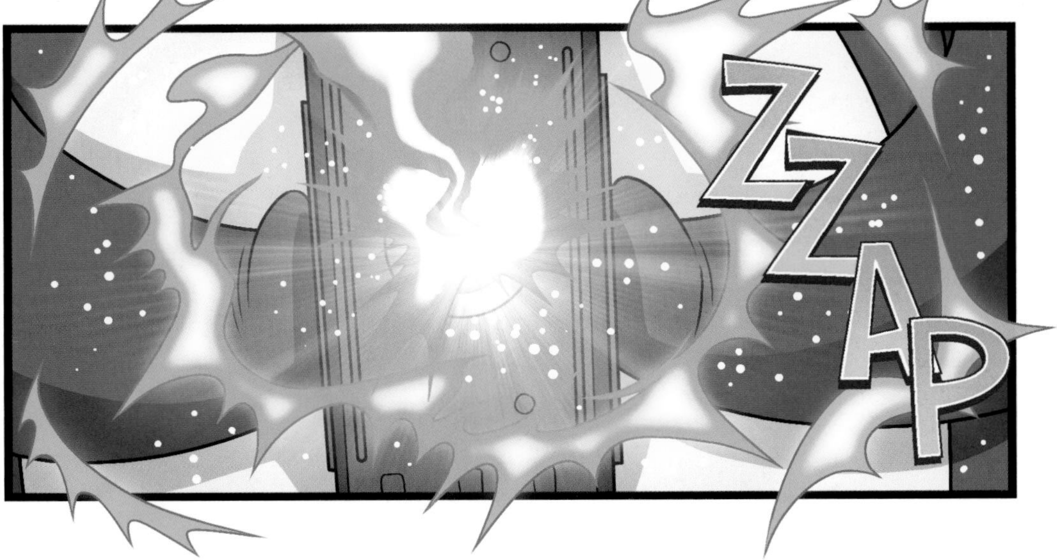
ZZAP

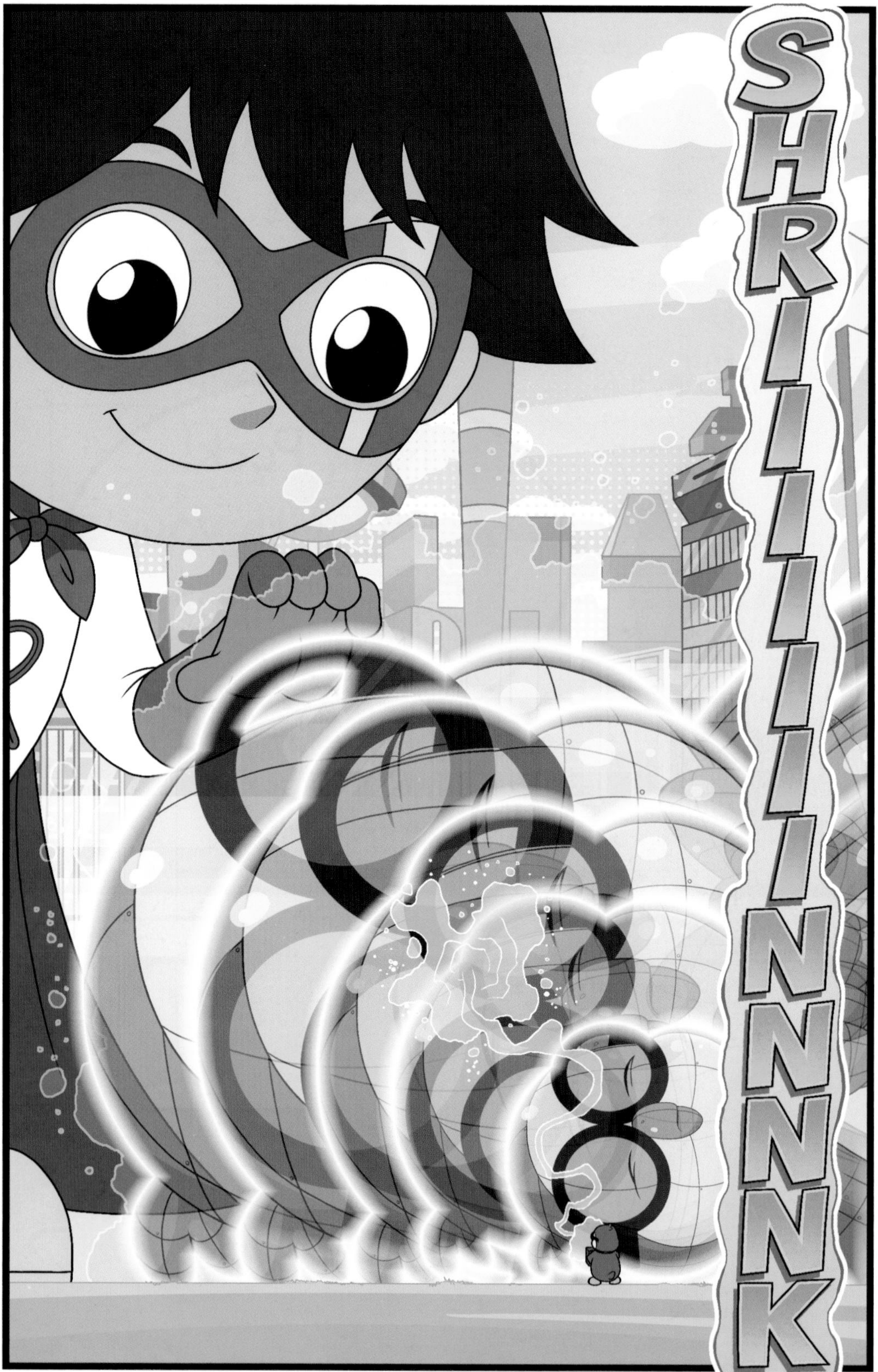
SHRIIIIINNNNK

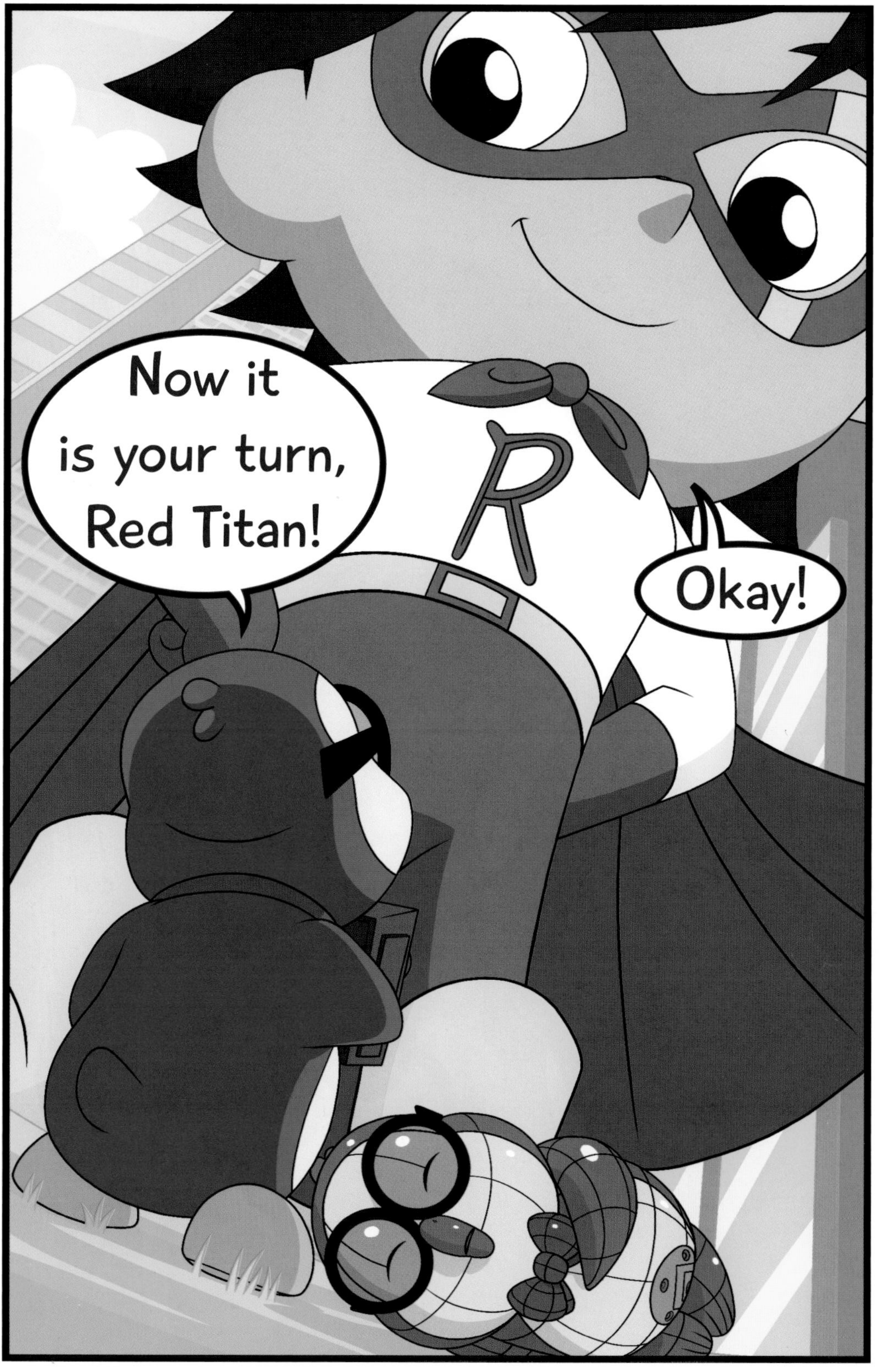
Now it is your turn, Red Titan!
Okay!

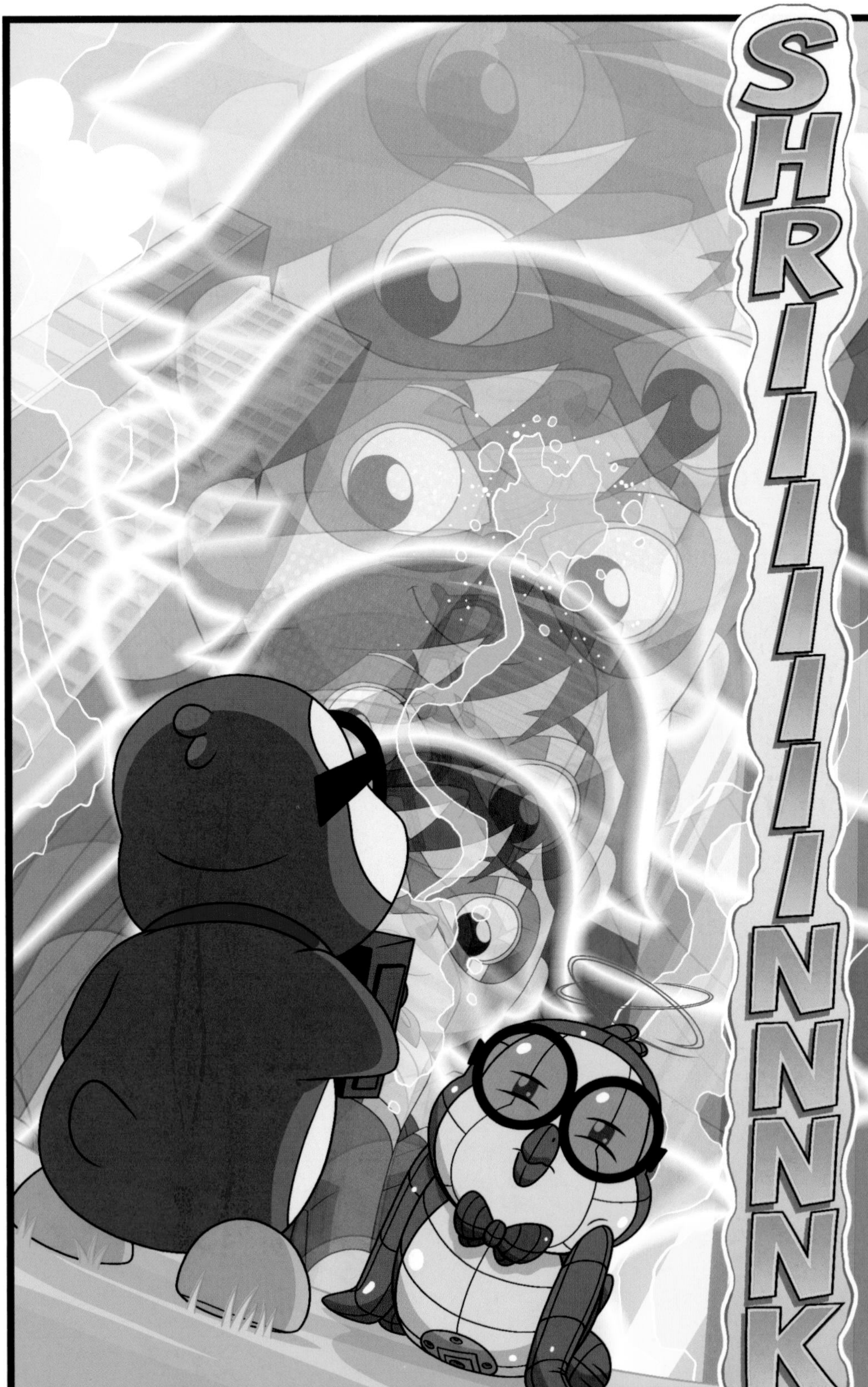
SHRIIIIIINNNNK

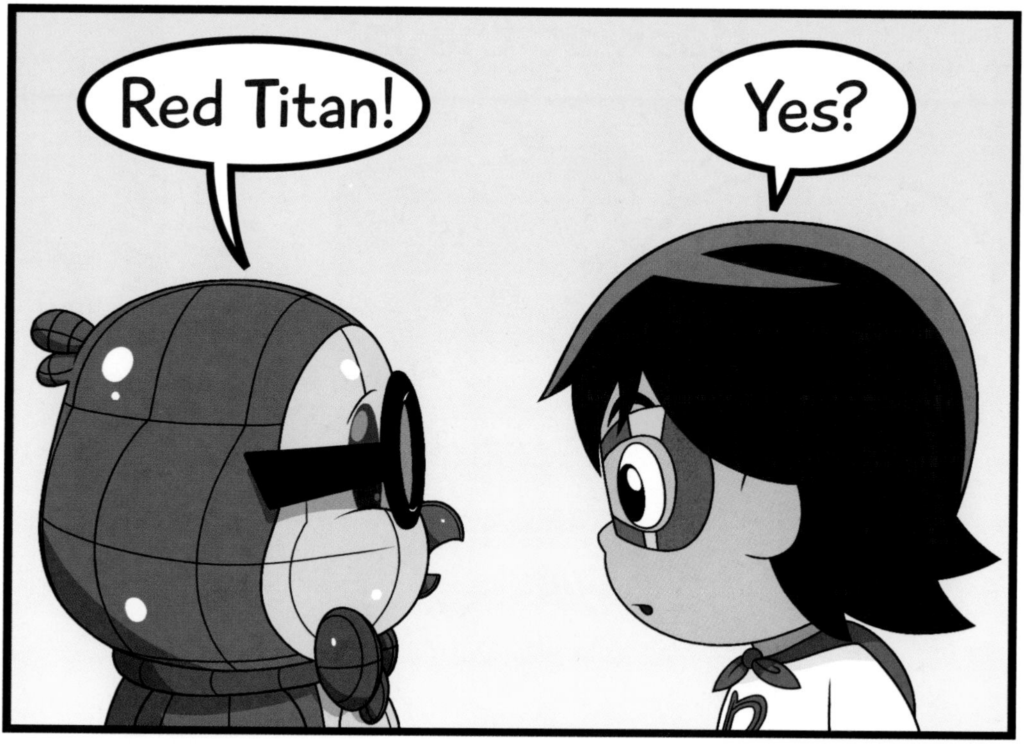
Red Titan!
Yes?

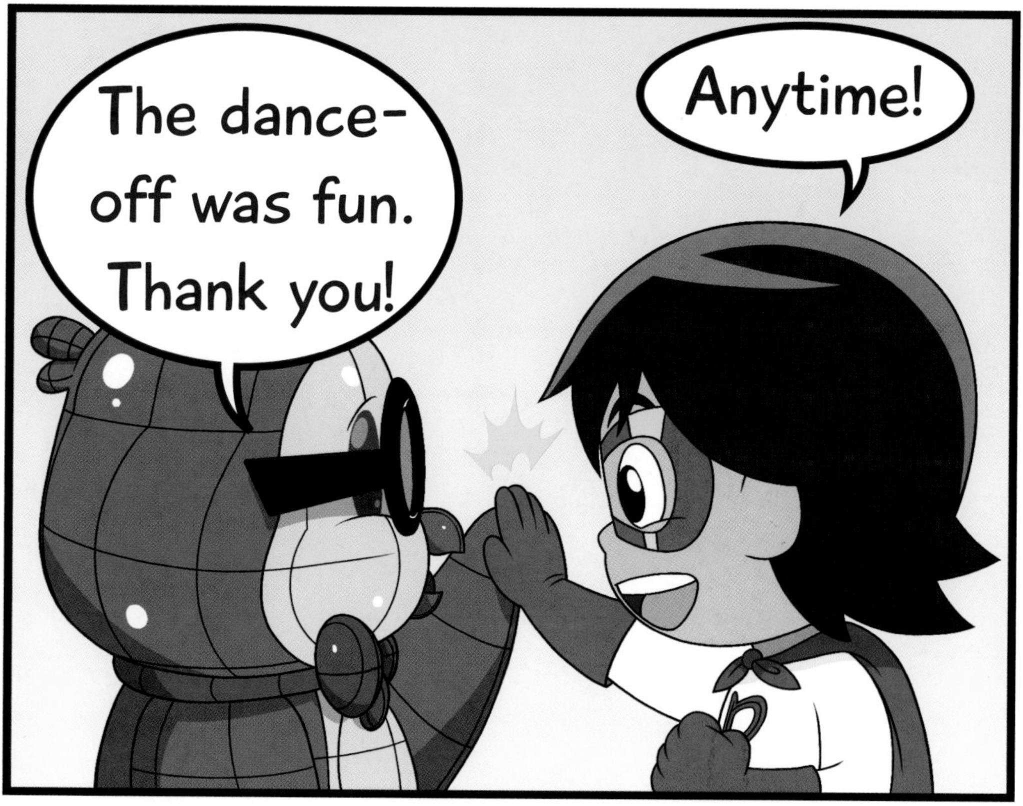
The dance-off was fun. Thank you!
Anytime!

Back at the lab...

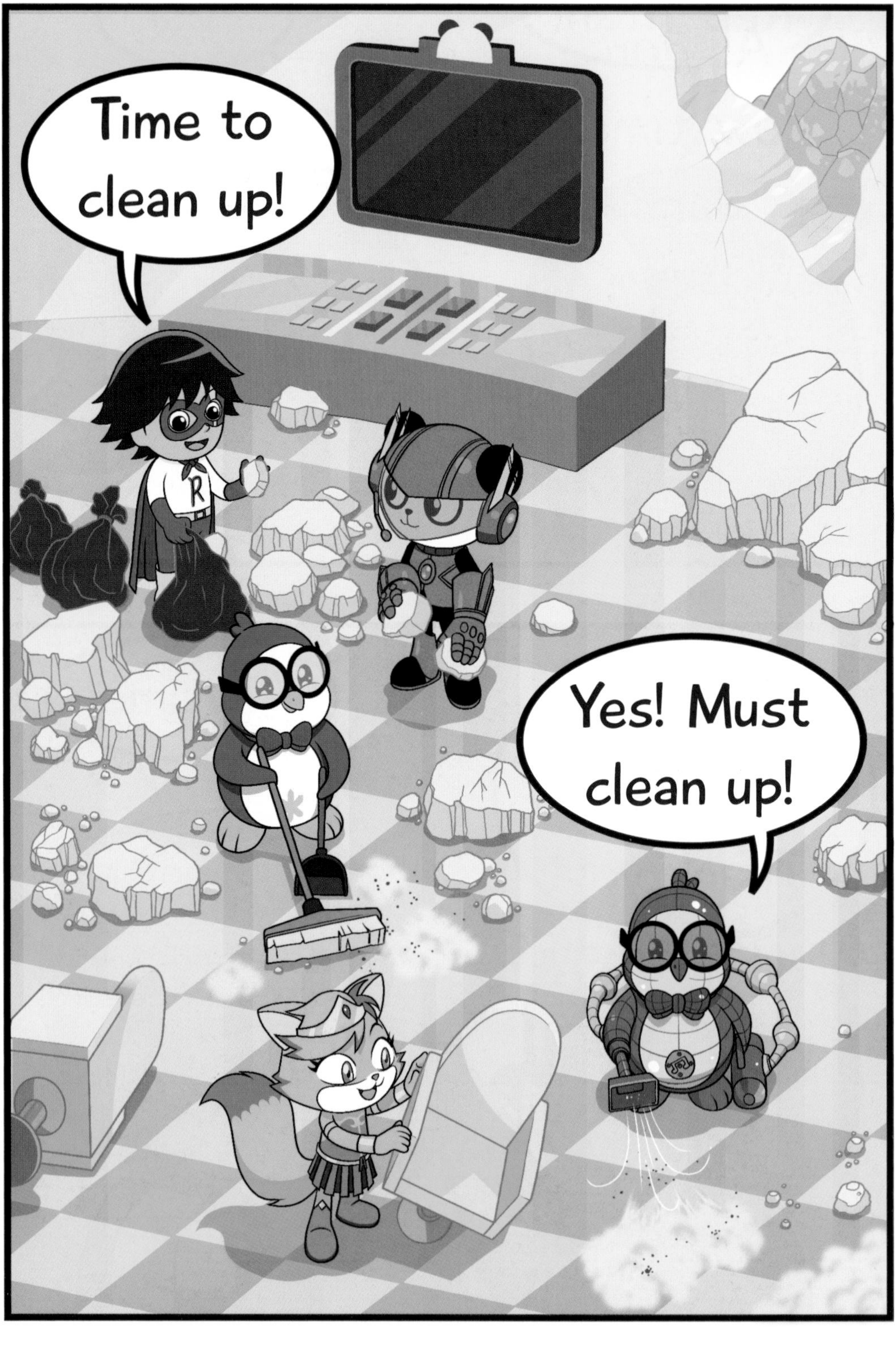
Time to clean up!
Yes! Must clean up!

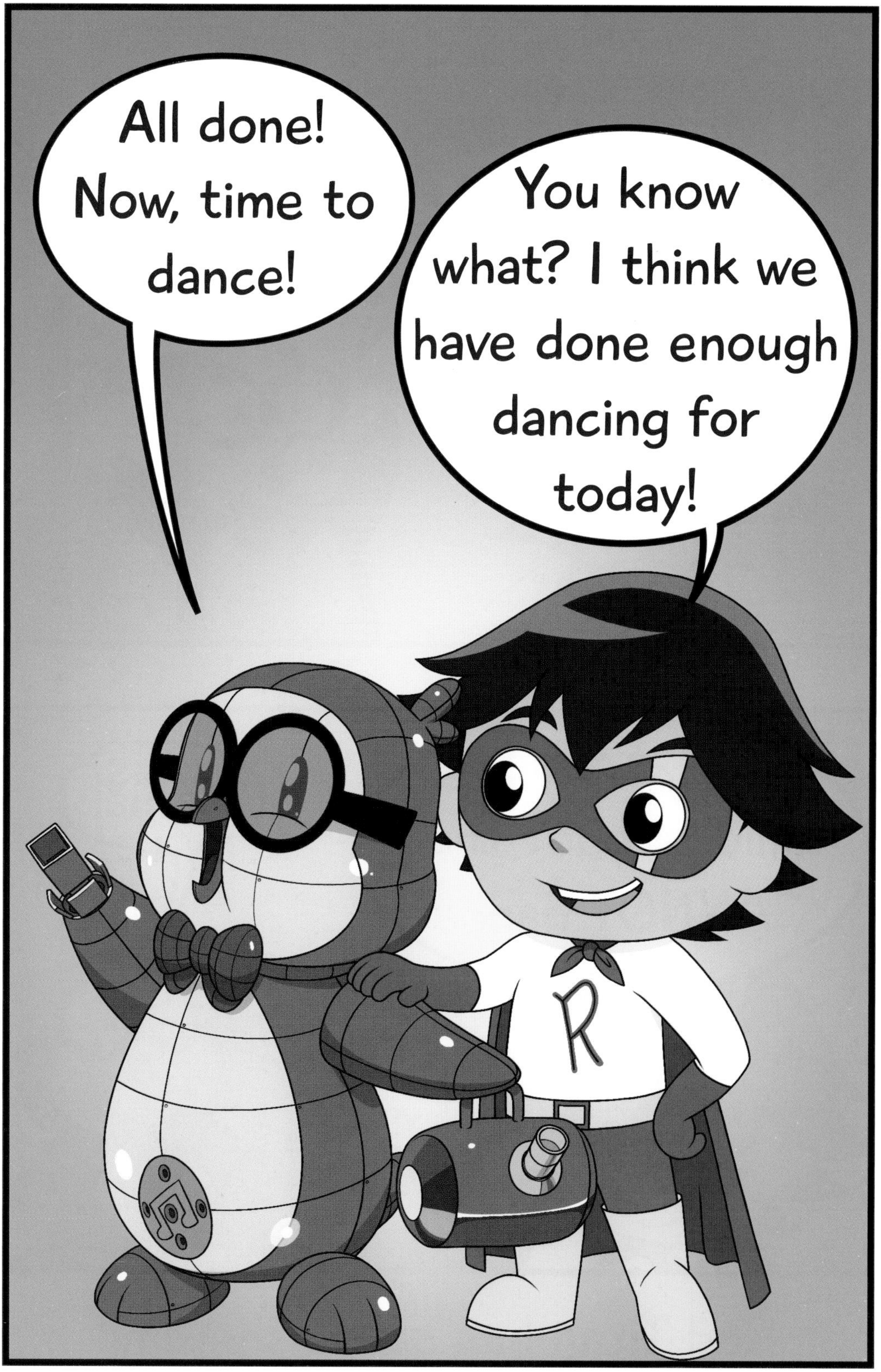
All done! Now, time to dance!
You know what? I think we have done enough dancing for today!

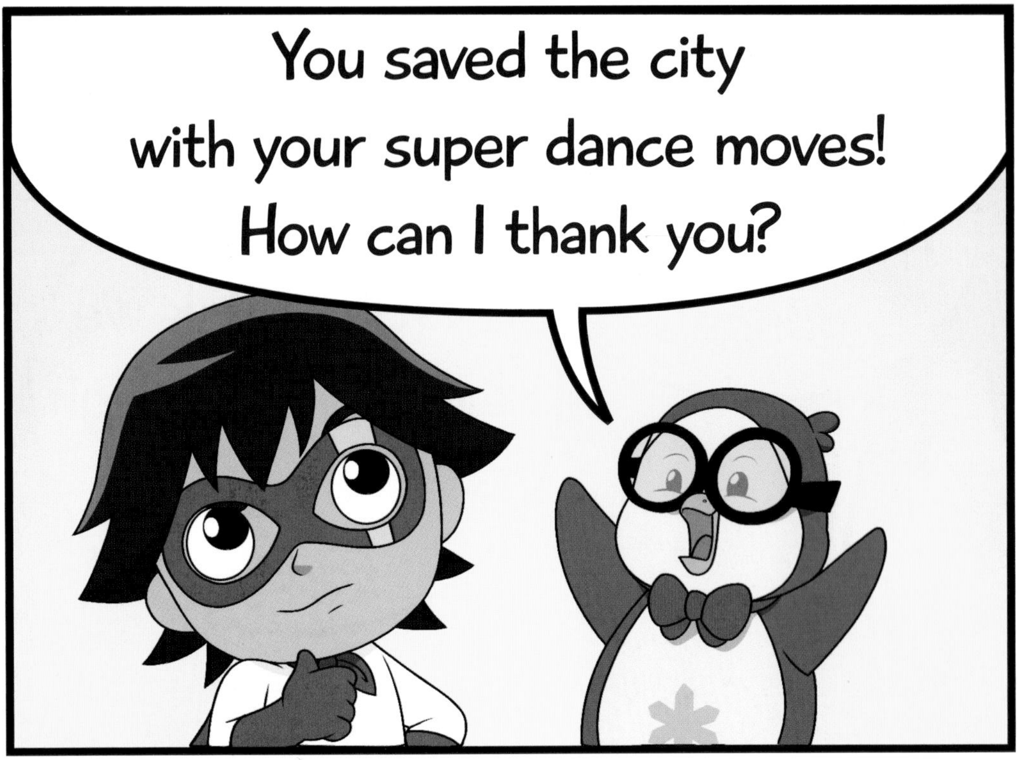
You saved the city with your super dance moves! How can I thank you?

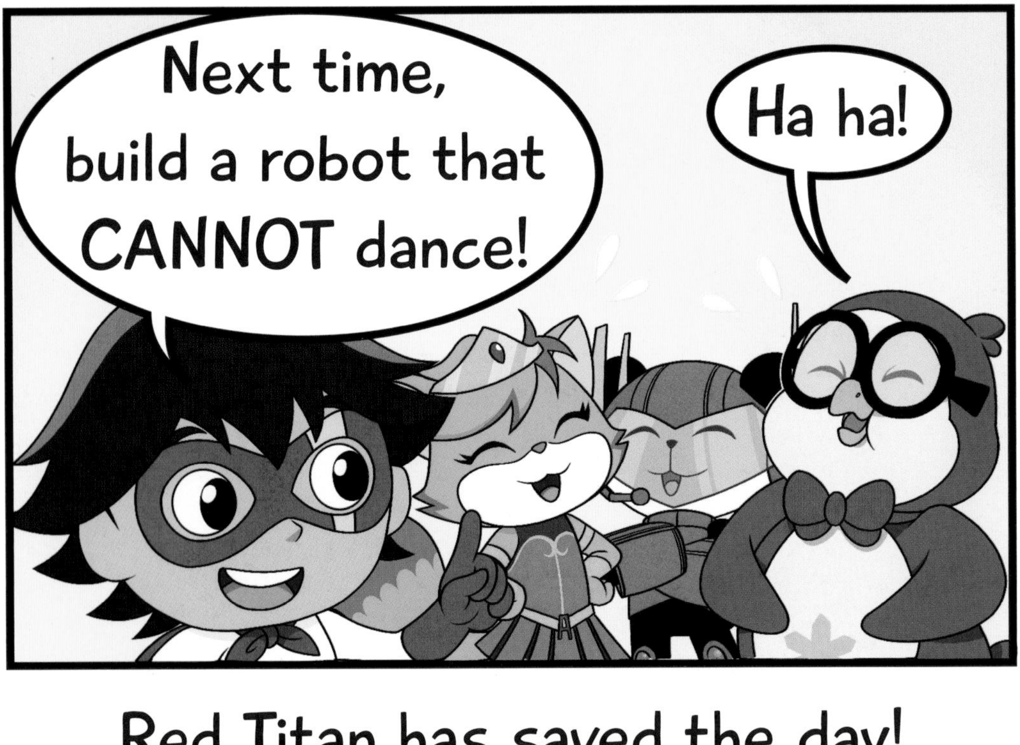
Next time, build a robot that CANNOT dance!
Ha ha!

Red Titan has saved the day!